# Bolan asked the FBI agent if he had a weapon

"I do," Tyler said, patting his chest.

"Better get ready. I think you're going to have to use it."

A dirty gray pickup truck whipped around the corner. The bed was filled with rough-looking men. The man in the passenger seat turned his pale, shaved head and yelled something at the driver. Two of the men in the back of the truck straightened and leveled AK-47s over the cab.

"Take cover!" Bolan yelled. "I'm going for those two tourists."

"Roger that," Grimaldi replied.

Bolan pulled out his Beretta 93R as he zigzagged through the picnic tables. "Get down!" he shouted at the French couple.

Bolan was about three steps from the tourists when the first rifle rounds zipped by him. He crouched and dove into the man, reaching out for the woman and pulling her down.

He counted eight men total from the truck, spread out across the plateau. The big bald guy, shouting orders in Russian, held his AK-47 over the truck's fender and sent a barrage at Grimaldi and Tyler, then aimed at Bolan. The picnic table's thick boards deflected the rounds. Bolan glanced back at the tourists. If they stayed there, hopefully they wouldn't get hit. He fired another three-round burst toward the truck.

Bolan saw the Russian guy smiling as he looked up over the top of his rifle.

# MACK BOLAN ®
## The Executioner

# THE EXECUTIONER

## DON PENDLETON'S

### DEADLY SALVAGE

A GOLD EAGLE BOOK FROM

# WORLDWIDE®

TORONTO • NEW YORK • LONDON
AMSTERDAM • PARIS • SYDNEY • HAMBURG
STOCKHOLM • ATHENS • TOKYO • MILAN
MADRID • WARSAW • BUDAPEST • AUCKLAND

First edition September 2014

ISBN-13: 978-0-373-64430-8

Special thanks and acknowledgment to
Michael A. Black for his contribution to this work.

DEADLY SALVAGE

**Printed in U.S.A.**

The sea does not belong to despots. On its surface immoral rights can still be claimed, men can fight each other, devour each other, and carry out all earth's atrocities. But thirty feet below the surface their power ceases, their influence fades, their authority disappears.

—Jules Verne,
*20,000 Leagues Under the Sea*

Land, sea or air, if an atrocity is about to be committed, I am duty-bound to stop it. There is no corner of this earth where criminals and despots will find impunity for their actions.
—Mack Bolan

# THE
# MACK BOLAN
## LEGEND

Nothing less than a war could have fashioned the destiny of the man called Mack Bolan. Bolan earned the Executioner title in the jungle hell of Vietnam.

But this soldier also wore another name—Sergeant Mercy. He was so tagged because of the compassion he showed to wounded comrades-in-arms and Vietnamese civilians.

Mack Bolan's second tour of duty ended prematurely when he was given emergency leave to return home and bury his family, victims of the Mob. Then he declared a one-man war against the Mafia.

He confronted the Families head-on from coast to coast, and soon a hope of victory began to appear. But Bolan had broken society's every rule. That same society started gunning for this elusive warrior—to no avail.

So Bolan was offered amnesty to work within the system against terrorism. This time, as an employee of Uncle Sam, Bolan became Colonel John Phoenix. With a command center at Stony Man Farm in Virginia, he and his new allies—Able Team and Phoenix Force—waged relentless war on a new adversary: the KGB.

But when his one true love, April Rose, died at the hands of the Soviet terror machine, Bolan severed all ties with Establishment authority.

Now, after a lengthy lone-wolf struggle and much soul-searching, the Executioner has agreed to enter an "arm's-length" alliance with his government once more, reserving the right to pursue personal missions in his Everlasting War.

# Prologue

Edwin Grimes watched the television monitor as the submersible's mechanical arm dipped around the ruptured hull of the sunken submarine, nimbly grabbing and tearing off some of the twenty centimeters of rubber covering. The massive, looping cables from the floating, semisubmersible platform held the sub in place. It amazed him that things looked so clear on the monitor at the depth of almost 3,000 meters, although wisps of silt from the seabed stirred up as the submersible altered its position. As soon as the area was monitored again for radiation, the divers could start the salvage process. Grimes turned to the technician at the console.

"What's the radiation level down there?"

The tech picked up the microphone and called the submersible.

"So far almost negligible," the dive leader replied. "We'll know more once we cut into the second hull."

Grimes looked at his watch. If they continued this operation through the night, they should be able to get into the compartments soon. He glanced out through the window. There was perhaps an hour of daylight left, but the sky was tinctured with a reddish glow. Grimes smiled.

Red sky by morning, sailor take warning. Red sky at night, sailor's delight. Or so the old saying went. He hoped the calm weather they'd been blessed with the past few weeks would indeed hold.

"Get the second dive team ready to go down in the bell," Grimes said. "Tell them to plan to stay submerged. That way they won't waste time decompressing each time."

The technician looked at him. "Is that wise, sir? We haven't got much daylight left."

Grimes turned to stare at the man. "Need I remind you I don't like to repeat myself?" He punctuated the question by removing the long, black leather sap he kept in his pocket, and placing the tip against the technician's jawline. The cords in the man's neck tightened.

Grimes smiled.

It was true, it would be dark soon, but at 3,000 meters below, what difference did that make? It was dark down there regardless, and the divers had to rely on artificial lighting. Grimes held the sap a moment longer, then let it drop. He said nothing more, but made a note to reprimand the salvage chief for placing such an idiot on the console. But that could wait, too. Everett would be expecting a full report when he came back to the island, but that wasn't for two more days. Grimes, however, was anxious to get off this floating platform rig and back on shore. "And tell them to get my boat ready. I'm going in."

The technician nodded and picked up the phone.

Good, Grimes thought. He knows he displeased me. Next time he'll be on his toes, or else his jaw will be wired shut.

Grimes left the control room and strolled around to the side of the platform, placing both hands on the metal safety railing and inhaling the fresh, salty air. The sun was an orange sphere, poised to descend into the ocean. It was a beautiful, awe-inspiring sight that never failed to please him. But something else caught his attention and broke the spell. A vessel was approaching, so close now that Grimes could see it was a luxury yacht. He turned and strode back into the control room.

"Check the monitors, you moron," he said. "I saw a ship out there."

The technician rolled his chair over to another section and nodded. "Yes, sir. Looks like a civilian yacht. A cabin cruiser, about fifty to sixty feet in length."

"Where the hell is that damn island police boat?"

The technician studied the radar screen and shook his head. "Can't place them, sir. Maybe they went to dinner."

Grimes swore under his breath. Those islanders were useless. What the hell was Everett paying them for? Still, at this point, the yacht situation might be better handled in-house. "Have a security team meet me by the launch immediately."

He turned and stormed out again, this time walking briskly down to the gangway that led to the lower section adjacent to one of the platform's massive buoyancy tanks. By the time Grimes reached the stairs to the launching platform, a squad of five men, all wearing sidearms and carrying AK-47 rifles, had hastily assembled, standing at attention. Grimes gave them a quick, cursory inspection. All had on their crisp, blue uniforms—BDU blouses and cargo pants—and they wore baseball hats emblazoned with Everett Security.

"We've got visitors," Grimes said, pointing to the yacht, which was perhaps five hundred yards away and still advancing. "The island police are nowhere to be found. We've got to do it ourselves."

Vincent Tanner, the security team leader, nodded and ordered his men to board a twenty-five-foot skiff. Grimes accompanied him to the cabin and watched as they fired up the engine and embarked on an intercept course. When they were about a hundred yards away, Grimes gave the order for the men below to keep their weapons out of sight for the time being. Then he picked up the microphone and called out over the loudspeaker, "You've entered a restricted area. Come to a stop immediately."

The yacht, which had *A Slice of Heaven* in black script along its prow, signaled with a blast from its horn, and slowed. Grimes scanned the wheelhouse, which was enclosed on three sides by glass windows under a sloping canopy. A middle-aged white guy with a glass in his hand, wearing a colorful shirt and a white captain's hat, stood next to a young Latino man at the yacht's controls. A woman in a bikini stood nearby, her body taut and very tan. The yacht was dead in the water now and Tanner cut the skiff's motor, letting them drift within shouting distance of the other vessel. The boat looked as if it could comfortably sleep at least four or five.

The white guy in the wheelhouse pushed back the window on one side and stuck his head out. "What the hell's all the yelling about?" His voice sounded thick.

"This is a restricted area," Grimes said. "You'll have to leave immediately."

"Restricted?" The man was slurring his words now, his movements slightly exaggerated. "Says who? You don't look like an official naval vessel to me. Besides, we're not even inside the three-mile limits yet. Are we?" He turned to the man at the wheel, who shrugged and smiled.

"Will you calm down, Harv?" the woman next to him said. She put her arm around the older man's shoulders and squeezed as she turned her head and flashed a smile at Grimes. "Good old Harv is a really nice guy," she called out. She was probably a little bit tipsy, too, but certainly less so than the man. "We didn't mean any harm, mister. We're headed for the main island to *par-ty.*"

Grimes figured her for her mid-to-late thirties. She had a nice body. Obviously, she had plenty of money to spend on cosmetic lifts, tucks and implants.

"Yeah," a guy on the lower deck yelled. He held up a camera with along zoom lens and clicked some pictures of the skiff and then of Grimes. "Say cheese. We've been filming you. I wanted to get some up-close shots of your rig over there." The camera's shutter clicked several more times as the man swiveled the lens from the skiff to the floating platform about a hundred yards away. "Got any good-looking girls on that thing could give me some nudie poses?"

"Oh, Norm, you're such a perv," a second woman, standing next to him, said. She gave his shoulder a playful slap.

These two looked drunk, as well.

"Hey," the cameraman said, still looking through the viewfinder. "You guys doing some kind of salvage operation over there?" He lowered his camera, pointing toward the platform. "Look at that. A submersible. Bigger than the one we used to use, Harv."

"Oh yeah?" Harv raised a set of binoculars to his eyes and studied the scene. "Well, I'll be damned. It sure is. We used to do underwater salvage. What's down there?"

Grimes's head whipped around. The second submersible was alongside the launch, and the divers were assembling as the crane arm hovered above them.

An unfortunate turn of events, thought Grimes. The last thing we need is a bunch of drunks shooting their mouths off about our operation at some island bar and showing photos. Especially if they know about salvage ops. He exhaled slowly, then said to Tanner in a low tone, "This has to be quick and neat."

Tanner nodded. He snapped off the safety on his AK-47, which he held down by his leg. "Ready when you are, sir."

"Take out the three above, but wait till I get aboard," Grimes said. "I'll take the other two."

Grimes stepped out onto the deck of the skiff and pulled on a pair of leather driving gloves. "Nice looking boat. How many does she hold?"

"Enough," Harv said, lowering the binoculars. His brow furrowed as Grimes reached for the ladder on the side of the yacht. "Hey, what are you doing?"

"Permission to come aboard," Grimes replied with a smile. He began to hoist himself up the ladder.

"I didn't say you could do that," Harv said, his drunken voice rising with the first vestiges of alarm. He turned to the young Latino. "Angel, get us out of here."

The man nodded and reached down toward a shiny silver lever.

A shot rang out. Angel's head jerked back, momentarily surrounded by a red halo, as a spiderweb of cracks sprang outward from the neat, round hole in the glass windshield. Harv's jaw dropped as a second shot pierced the glass, and he grabbed his chest as he dropped. The tan woman started to scream. A third shot burst into the wheelhouse. Her voice ceased as she fell.

Grimes was at the top of the ladder now and going over the side. He drew his Heckler and Koch 9 millimeter and aimed at Norm, who was frozen in place on the stern. Grimes double-tapped the trigger, sending two rounds into his chest. Norm lurched forward, clutching the growing red stain expanding over the front of his crisp white shirt. The woman next to him was paralyzed for a moment, too, but as he collapsed she turned and ran toward the cabin doors.

"You've got no place to go," Grimes said. The next round from his H&K caught her in the side and she flopped onto the deck, squirming and crying as her long legs kicked.

Not bad for a one-handed shot, thought Grimes as he assumed a two-handed grip and aimed carefully before sending his next round directly into her left temple. The screaming stopped abruptly and a trickle of blood flowed from her open mouth.

Grimes leaped down onto the deck, immediately moved to the cabin doors and kicked them open. A quick search revealed no other passengers. He surveyed the interior. Nice flat-screen television, a wet bar, and three separate sleeping quarters on either side. Tanner appeared in the doorway, holding out his hand.

"Here's your brass. And their camera."

Grimes holstered his H&K, placed the spent shell casings in his pocket and began to review the digital photos. Most of them showed the now-departed crew in a variety of poses. Obviously, they were exhibitionists, but that didn't matter now. They'd been a security risk, pure and simple. The boss would probably not be happy, but he would no doubt approve.

The camera also contained several clear shots of Grimes, Tanner, the divers and the submersible. Grimes started to press the delete button, but hesitated. Perhaps these would be worth showing to Everett when he got here in case he was miffed at the shooting. He was going to want a full briefing, and this way it would contain visual aids. Grimes smiled at his wit as he slung the camera strap over his neck. "Leave some men here to secure this boat. Find their passports. After you take me back, return here and go through it with a fine-tooth comb. Dump everything of value overboard. Then set this thing adrift far away from here. Make it look like the work of pirates, or drug smugglers or something."

"Understood, sir," Tanner said.

Grimes climbed the steps and strode past the two bodies, which were still leaking bright crimson onto the pristine whiteness of the lower deck. He hesitated, but couldn't resist taking a few photos of his handiwork. He turned and snapped a few of good old Harv, his pretty lady, and the dead Latino kid, as well.

A bit of an untidy mess, but necessary for the mission, Grimes thought as he stepped over them. Collateral damage.

# 1

Mack Bolan, also known as the Executioner, passed the three-mile marker and noted that he had finally broken a sweat. He carried a five-pound dumbbell in each hand. The trees and bushes on either side of the macadamized track that led through the heavily wooden area surrounding Stony Man Farm had just started to sprout their seasonal leaves. Bright sunshine filtered through the swirls of green buds, dappling the trail ahead with splashes of brilliance. Running this five-mile course was a great way to unwind after returning from a mission. Up ahead, two deer walked across the path, stopped, saw Bolan and scampered into the forest.

Suddenly, a distant but distinct buzzing began to intrude on the peaceful scene. The birds became silent as the buzzing grew louder. Bolan had already identified it: a motorcycle—a trail bike most likely—and it was heading his way. Although the soldier normally felt totally comfortable and safe within the confines of Stony Man Farm, his survival instinct never allowed him to completely drop his guard. The trail curved to the left and he quickened his pace, sprinting around the turn, at once out of view from the approaching motorcyclist. He slowed and waded into the heavy foliage. Stopping next to an oak tree, he dropped the dumbbells and pulled his SIG Sauer P938 Nightmare from the pocket of his sweatpants. Then he waited.

When Bolan heard the motorcycle slowing to make the turn, he brought the SIG up and braced his arm against the heavy trunk. The motorcycle rider accelerated and zoomed past Bolan's position, only to slow down and screech to a halt about eight seconds later.

The rider removed his helmet, but Bolan had already identified him.

It was Jack Grimaldi. Bolan lowered the pistol, grabbing the weights with his left hand and stepping out of the trees.

Grimaldi swiveled in the seat. "Are you slipping or something?" he asked. "You made more noise than a troop of Boy Scouts."

"I'll give back my merit badge."

Grimaldi's eyebrows rose as he looked at the pistol. "Where's your Beretta? It's not like you to be without your baby."

"Sometimes less is more when it comes to concealment," Bolan said. He pocketed the SIG, took a dumbbell in each hand and began running again.

Grimaldi twisted the accelerator and pulled up beside Bolan. "Hal sent me to get you."

"Well, you got me."

The pilot smiled. "Come on, he wants to see you right away."

Bolan kept running.

"Did you hear me?" Grimaldi asked. "He said 'right away.'"

"I heard. Tell him I'll be there shortly."

"Hop on and I'll give you a ride."

"Nope," Bolan said. "I've been promising myself this run ever since I got back. I'll be there in twenty minutes."

"Twenty minutes? You slowed down that much?"

"I can make it quicker if I skip my shower," Bolan said drily.

Grimaldi grinned. "We wouldn't want that. See you later." He stopped, replaced the helmet on his head, and asked, "Want to race?"

Bolan didn't answer, and seconds later Grimaldi zoomed past him with a spray of gravel.

BOLAN WALKED INTO the War Room freshly showered and changed. Hal Brognola glanced up from his big desk. "Have a nice run?"

"Pretty good until you and Jack ruined it. What's up?"

"We may have something brewing in the Caribbean."

"Like what?"

"Missing yacht, for one thing," Brognola said. "A bunch of rich folks out of Miami. Big campaign contributors to a lot of politicians on the Hill. They took off for the islands and haven't been heard from in two days."

"Sounds like a job for the Coast Guard."

"Normally, it would be," Brognola said. "But there may be more to it. The FBI's also nosing around down there on one of the islands. Something about a missing DOD employee."

Bolan felt his interest spike slightly at that news. In the old days, a missing Department of Defense employee often meant a defection. Now, it could mean terrorism. "What type of employee?"

Brognola picked up a manila file and passed it across his desk. "The guy's worked there as a crypto code breaker for just about forever. Never had any problems. His name's Herman Monk."

Bolan paged through the file. A color photo of Monk was paper-clipped to the inside of the folder. It showed a middle-aged man with thinning hair and thick, horn rim glasses. Other than that, his face was unremarkable. Under the personal information section he was listed as fifty-eight years old and widowed with one child, a nineteen-year-old daughter named Grace. A picture of her was on a subsequent page.

"As I said," Brognola continued, "Monk's worked at the DOD for a long time, since the Cold War. He's an expert crypto analyst. Speaks five languages. He's supposed to be a wizard at breaking codes, but he hasn't had a lot to do since the Soviet Union dissolved. He used to track the Soviets around the globe, and more recently the activities of Al Qaeda and friends."

"The Feds got any theories?"

"He disappeared from work four days ago. Left for a lunch date and never returned. He called in sick for the rest of that day and the next. It was later discovered that he was in the possession of his government laptop." Brognola got up, went to the coffeemaker on the file cabinet and poured himself a cup. "When Monk didn't show up for work the following day, they tried calling him, but kept getting his answering machine saying he was still sick. Then they traced the laptop through the built-in GPS transmitter and went to his residence. The laptop was there, but its hard drive wasn't. And neither was Monk."

"What type of information was on it?" Bolan asked.

"Unknown," Brognola said. "Most of Monk's work these days was translating intercepted texts from Arabic. Like I said, he speaks five languages in addition to English. Arabic, Farsi, Russian, Korean and several Chinese dialects."

"He should apply for a job at the United Nations."

Brognola took a sip of his coffee and returned to his desk. "They traced him to a flight three days ago to Puerto Rico."

"Maybe he wants to be there for the vice president's visit."

"That's not for a few more days," Brognola said. "Anyway, from there it's believed he hopped another flight to one of the Caribbean islands."

"Which one?"

"This one, we think. St. Francis." Brognola handed Bolan a brightly colored brochure depicting beautiful hotels rising out of white sand, and photos of equally beautiful people drinking and playing volleyball in bikinis and Speedos. "At least that's what the Feds think. The FBI is down there now trying to find him and his daughter."

"His daughter?" Bolan flipped the file open again and looked at the girl's picture.

"Yeah, she was down there a week ago. Apparently, she won some kind of free, all-inclusive vacation. Checked into her hotel and hasn't been seen since."

"So you're thinking the girl might have been kidnapped?"

"Again, unknown, but if Monk has been traced to the same island, it could be a bit more than coincidence. There seem to be a lot of Americans going missing down that way. It's the same general vicinity where the yacht disappeared." He handed Bolan another file, which contained pictures of two couples, a young Hispanic man and a luxury yacht with *A Slice of Heaven* emblazoned on the front.

"So why not let the Feds handle it?" Bolan asked. "Why do we need to get involved?"

"You know how the President feels about checks and balances. He's not totally comfortable letting the FBI be the only player in the game down there. They can tend to get kind of uptight and formal, especially when they're investigating something in a foreign country. Sticklers about following the rules. So who better than us to be an impartial observer?"

"Yeah, right."

"Oh, and I should mention," Brognola said. "They're making some kind of blockbuster movie down there, financed by none other than Willard Forsythe Everett III. He's also hosting the Mr. Galaxy contest on the island this weekend."

"Does this mean he's not going to run for president again?"

Brognola chuckled. "He's got enough money to, but apparently he's got a new agenda. The island belongs to the French and Dutch, but Everett built an enormous hotel resort there called the Omni. That's where you'd be staying. Word is, he's planning on turning the entire island into an adult playground."

"And do you think he has anything to do with the Monk situation?"

"Hard to say," Brognola answered. "But I'd like you to keep an eye on things at the Omni, as well. We'll be sending along someone to accompany you as part of your cover."

"Who?"

"Jack." Brognola grinned. "So, you interested?"

"I'm game," Bolan replied.

GRIMES WATCHED WILLARD FORSYTHE EVERETT III finish going through the digital images on the camera. Everett was sitting on a sumptuous sofa in the massive penthouse suite atop the Omni hotel. Everett wasn't a big man by normal standards, but he always carried himself as if he were six feet four. In reality, he was more like five-eight or -nine, depending on the size of the lifts in his shoes.

But there was no denying that he was in incredible

shape. He wore a short-sleeved polo shirt and the muscles in his arms rippled with each movement. He regularly worked out with full-contact karate fighters and boxers. His latest kick was the Mixed Martial Arts stuff, but Grimes figured that was because he could keep hitting people after he had them down. Of course, those sparring with Everett knew better than to try too hard to win. The boss didn't like to lose. He had a bit of what was traditionally referred to as a "Napoleon complex."

Everett turned off the camera and stood, tossing it next to the pile of papers on his large desk. He walked over to the open patio doors overlooking the beach, and clasped his hands behind his back.

"Those broads were kind of good-looking," he said. "Too bad you had to eliminate them."

Grimes waited for Everett's further comment on the tactical neutralization of the people on the yacht, but the billionaire didn't seem that concerned. Collateral damage had been an accurate assessment on Grimes's part, after all. Everett looked tired, though. Grimes knew the rich bastard had just returned from receiving his biannual regimen of steroid and hormone treatments that allowed him to maintain his youthful constitution as he crested middle age. Hair transplants, cosmetic tucks, hormone shots, cheek implants.... Maybe Everett was contemplating another run for the White House.

"What's the status of the recovery?" he asked.

"I've had the men working twenty-four/seven," Grimes said. "We've cut through the second hull, but we have to constantly monitor the radiation levels."

"Understandable," Everett allowed, "but the clock's ticking. Remember I'm juggling the timing of the takeover of the *Xerxes,* too. It was just getting to Cuba when I left for my treatments."

"It's on its way back now," Grimes said. "Near the Isla de Margarita. We're tracking it by satellite, waiting till it gets past Tobago before we make our move."

"Where's Tanner?"

"Went to Jamaica yesterday to tag up with the Russians. They're tracking the *Xerxes* and will intercept with the helicopter from there, once it gets into the Caribbean."

Everett's face twisted into a frown. "Is Zelenkov sure he can handle it?"

"He's ex-Spetsnaz and was fully trained in ship assaults. The Iranians will never know what hit them."

Everett nodded, but blew out a long breath. "Everything has to coincide exactly, without…creating too many waves." He paused and smiled at his own pun. "And imagine me playing on the same team as the Ruskies. Who would have thought?" He laughed.

Grimes forced a laugh, too. This seemed to please the boss. Good. The last thing he wanted to do was piss the guy off. His temper was legendary.

"What about those FBI agents?" Everett asked.

"Most of them are in Ponce helping check things out for the vice president's visit."

Everett smiled. "They won't know what hit 'em. What about the agent they sent here?"

"Just a big, dumb Iowa farm boy. He's being led around by one of Le Pierre's goons on a snipe hunt."

"We can't assume that'll last forever." Everett glanced at his watch. "Okay, line up a couple sparring partners for me. I want to work out before we go out on the rig." He strode back to the desk and picked up the camera.

"Want me to delete those pics?" Grimes asked.

Everett rotated his head, as if loosening up his neck

muscles. "Not till I tell you. Keep me posted on the salvage progress, and keep your eyes open for any new arrivals. Especially Americans."

## 2

The airport was on the southern, Dutch side of the island and situated uncomfortably close to the populated beach. Grimaldi remarked that a high serve from one of the beach volleyball games could have bounced off the big 747's window as they skidded onto the tarmac and began braking to a stop.

"It looks pretty tight, all right," Bolan said. "Maybe that's why they booked us commercial instead of having you try to fly us down."

"Like hell." Grimaldi frowned. "I could've landed this tub so smoothly it would have been like flopping down onto a featherbed."

Bolan grinned. His old friend always prided himself on being able to fly anything with wings or rotors better than anyone else. And he was probably right.

As the two of them stood in the customs line for arriving passengers, the soldier looked around. Their line was full of tourist groups and was moving at a snail's pace, compared to the one on their right, which moved faster but was considerably longer. Grimaldi seemed to notice this, too.

"The line you're in always seems to move slowest, doesn't it?" he said.

Bolan nodded as he studied the makeup of the other

line. It was overwhelmingly composed of black and Hispanic people with makeshift luggage. They weren't dressed like tourists, and seemed to be conversing in either Spanish or French.

Prospective workers, Bolan thought, probably from the Dominican Republic, Puerto Rico or Haiti.

He looked at the customs agent scrutinizing the passports and papers. The man waved one arrival through and accepted a passport from the next person. Bolan watched as the agent opened the passport, holding it up in front of him, then quickly rubbed his hand over it. A quick cough followed and he brought his right palm up to cover his mouth. Then he dipped his hand beneath the counter, appearing to wipe it on his pant leg. He asked a few more questions and then waved the person through the gate.

As their line progressed Bolan watched the man repeat the coughing gesture, or a variation of it, sometimes using a sneeze, with four other arriving passengers. Bolan was close enough to read the agent's name tag now: J. Van der Hyden.

Grimaldi was next in line and stepped forward, handing over his passport with an exasperated, "Finally."

The customs agent smiled pleasantly and gave a welcome greeting in accented English. "And what, may I ask, is the purpose of your visit?"

"You may ask," Grimaldi said, gesturing toward Bolan and himself. "We're reporters. My partner and I are here to cover the big movie that Willard Everett III is producing down here."

"Ah, yes," the agent said. "That is on the French side. May I see your passport, as well, sir?"

Bolan handed the man his passport, which was under the name Matt Cooper, his civilian alias. The agent's eyes went from Grimaldi to Bolan, then back to their passports as he shone a light on both documents, making a thorough examination.

Two more people slipped through the gate from Van der Hyden's line.

The customs agent looked up at them once more. "You may pick up your luggage at the end of the corridor. Have a pleasant stay on the island."

Grimaldi grabbed the passports and handed Bolan his. "Took him long enough," the pilot said as they headed to the luggage carousel. "Did you see how many people got through the other station before us?"

"There's a reason for that," Bolan replied. "Most of them had a c-note in their passports. They're probably here illegally."

Grimaldi smirked. "Hey, so are we, in a manner of speaking."

THE ROAD WOUND through the mountains, widening occasionally on fenced-off plateaus where numerous taxis had pulled over and parked so tourists could take pictures of the scenic view. After Bolan and Grimaldi rented a car at the airport, a Citroën, they'd loaded their luggage into the trunk and taken off toward their hotel, which was on the French side of the island. Bolan let the pilot drive, and as the cool wind whipped through the open window, checked in for a sitrep with Brognola on his satellite phone .

"How's it going so far?" the big Fed asked.

"Not bad," Bolan said. "We're on our way to the Omni now."

"Good to hear," Brognola said. "We're working on hooking you guys up with the FBI agent down there."

The curving roadway straightened out and they started a descent. Ahead, Bolan could see the bay area, with numerous high-rise hotels blocking out the view of the ocean beyond. The tallest one, he knew from his research, was Everett's resort. Between the ridge they were on and the wall of hotels was a sea of ramshackle buildings and houses where he assumed the locals lived.

Catching a glimpse of something in the side mirror, Bolan straightened. A white jeep was behind them, with POLICE stenciled in black block letters below the windshield. Its flashers lit up and a siren began to wail.

"Hal, I'll call you back," Bolan said. "We've got a slight problem."

"What kind of problem?"

"Island police," Bolan said. "Jack must have been speeding."

Grimaldi swore as he pulled the rental car over to the side of the road and stopped. "I'm liking this place less and less," he said as he and Bolan exited the vehicle.

Two officers approached. One was a tall, muscular black man with a neatly trimmed beard and a starched blue-and-white uniform with chevrons on the shoulders. The other man was white, about five foot eight, and sported a pencil-thin mustache. His uniform had a row of shiny gold buttons, a three-stripe captain's insignia on both epaulets and a golden braid looped through the left one. His name tag read LE PIERRE.

Bolan studied the sidearms that both men wore. The sergeant's was a Manurhin MR 73 .357 Magnum revolver. The captain's weapon looked to be a 9 mm SIG Sauer SP2022. Both dependable guns with smooth action. Bolan smiled. "Good afternoon, Officers. What can we do for you?"

"Ah." The captain lifted an eyebrow. "You are Americans, *n'est-ce pas*?"

"That's right," Grimaldi said. "How can we help you?"

"You will both give your passports to the sergeant," the captain said.

Bolan and Grimaldi handed over their documents. The big man glared at them and handed the passports to Le Pierre, who took his time paging through them. "No luggage?"

"It's in the trunk," Bolan said.

"Open it immediately, Gipardieu." He uttered the rest of his instructions to the sergeant in French, and Bolan gathered that Gipardieu had been directed to search their luggage.

"We already went through customs," Grimaldi said. "What's the problem here?"

"*Here*, as you say, is the problem." The captain took another step forward so that his face was only a few inches from Grimaldi's. "You are now in French territory."

Bolan saw Grimaldi's face start to redden. "Jack," he barked. "Just open the trunk."

His mouth set in a firm line, Grimaldi turned and opened the rear compartment of the Citroën.

The big man stepped forward. "Move aside," he said. His voice sounded high and whiny for such a huge man.

Bolan and Grimaldi exchanged looks and stepped back.

Sergeant Gipardieu took out the three bags, moved around to the side of the car and set them on the roof. He unzipped the two suitcases and fingered through the clothes and toiletries. Then he opened the third case, which had a hard outer shell and silver clasps.

"Be careful with that," Grimaldi said. "It's fragile."

Gipardieu hesitated.

"What is it?" Captain Le Pierre asked.

"It's our camera and video equipment," Bolan said. "We're magazine reporters. We're here to do a story on the new movie being filmed, and the Mr. Galaxy contest."

Le Pierre muttered something else in French and made a quick motion with his hand, adding "*Vite, vite.*"

Bolan watched as Gipardieu took the cameras, camcorder and various attachments out of their foam encasements.

"And what is this?" The captain pointed to a pair of angular handles with grooved, flat metal tops.

"Those are handles for our camcorder," Bolan said.

Le Pierre studied the items, then blinked a few times.

"Captain," Bolan said, "can we do anything else for you? If not, it was a very long flight, and my partner and I would like to check into our hotel and relax a bit."

Le Pierre raised his eyes from the case and studied Bolan's face for several seconds. He glanced down at the passports and then up again. "Monsieur Cooper…"

Bolan waited. Had their cover been blown? Did this guy know them from somewhere?

Le Pierre gestured to Gipardieu, who slammed the camera case closed. The sergeant turned and walked back to Le Pierre, leaving the three bags on the roof. Le Pierre handed the passports back to Grimaldi and Bolan.

"It is my hope that you enjoy your stay here, *messieurs*," he said. The two officers began to walk back to their jeep. "*Au revoir.*"

"What an asshole," Grimaldi said as they reloaded their bags and climbed back into the Citroën.

"Oh, I don't know," Bolan said. "You and he have might have more in common than you think."

"Yeah? Like what?"

"Well, I know you have a thing for pretty French girls." Bolan settled himself into the seat. "And it looks like you both share a preference for SIG Sauers."

Grimaldi slammed the Citroën into gear and peeled out.

**3**

Bolan dialed Brognola back on the sat phone as they pulled into the Omni hotel's parking lot. "What's the latest on that hookup with the Feds?" Bolan asked after he'd filled Brognola in on their encounter with the local police.

"Should be all set," Brognola said. "I'll email you the agent's info and sat phone number. We're trying to finalize a meeting time now. I'll send the location as soon as I get it. I've also arranged all of your hardware—it will be delivered directly to the hotel. And I'll see if Aaron can run a check on Le Pierre and that Dutch customs agent. What was his name again?"

"J. Van der Hyden." Bolan spelled it.

"Got it. I'll get back to you."

"Roger that," Bolan said.

He ended the call. Inside the main lobby, the clerk behind the polished teakwood counter was all smiles and efficiency. He offered them complimentary drink passes to the beach bar, and snapped his fingers at a bellman, telling him to carry the luggage up to their room.

They stepped into an elevator with a glass wall that gave them a postcard perfect view of the beach and ocean. As they rose to the fourth floor, Bolan could see numerous piers with boats of various sizes tethered to the moorings.

"They have boats over there to go fishing and diving?" he asked.

The bellman nodded and flashed a wide smile. "Yes, sir. Fishing, diving, waterskiing, paragliding, anything you want. The concierge can arrange it for you. If you wish, I can have him call up to your room."

Bolan and Grimaldi exchanged looks. Special attention was not what they wanted right now.

"Maybe later," Grimaldi said. The elevator stopped and they moved down the hallway toward their room. It faced the ocean, and was much closer to the stairway than the elevator. Good for slipping in and out without drawing too much attention.

"These bags are a bit heavier than they look, sir," the bellman said.

"Give the kid a nice tip, Matt," Grimaldi said as he stuck the key card into the slot. "He's earned it."

Bolan tipped the bellman, who continued to offer assistance in procuring anything, anything at all, that they might desire, including an introduction to some beautiful island girls who liked Americans.

Bolan declined and closed the door.

"Not so fast," Grimaldi said. "That last part about the island girls sounded kind of interesting."

"We're here to work," Bolan said drily.

The room was fairly expansive, with two beds, a wet bar built into one wall, and a lounge area. The drapes on the window were open, offering a perfect view of the ocean side.

Bolan secured the dead bolt lock as he and Grimaldi continued their innocuous conversation about the nice flight and the pleasant drive from the airport. As they talked, Bolan pulled out his bug detection scanner and searched the room for any type of listening or recording devices. The scanner detected bugs in the bedroom, bathroom and lounge area.

Grimaldi picked up the phone, dialing the main desk. "I'm sorry, this room won't do," he said as soon as the clerk answered.

"Is there a problem, sir?"

"Yeah," he said. "There's a strange smell in here, and my partner is very sensitive."

The clerk hemmed and hawed a bit, but when Grimaldi threatened to vacate the room and send an email to the bureau of travel and tourism, the man agreed to send up the bellman to show them to another suite.

"Tell him to hurry up," he said. "My partner's getting nauseous and has a tendency to throw up when he gets a whiff of something rotten."

After five minutes of waiting, Grimaldi repeated his call to the front desk, this time inserting a bit more anger and outrage into his tone. The bellman's knock came approximately a minute later. It was the same one as before, and he was carrying a large, locked suitcase.

"Delivery for you, sir," he said to Bolan.

Bolan thanked him and grabbed the heavy case, giving it a quick once-over for signs of tampering. This had to be the weapons and gear Brognola had arranged a CIA contact to secure and drop off for them. The bellman picked up the remaining three bags and showed the men to another room on the same floor, at the opposite side of the building. It was close to a second stairwell. Grimaldi went in, checked it out and came back into the hall with a smile.

"This one looks more suitable," he said, grabbing the camera case. "Tip the kid, will you, Matt?"

Bolan gave him some more money. "Here's hoping we don't see you again today."

The bellman looked down at the bills and flashed a big

grin. "Oh, I don't mind, sir. Not at all." He placed the bags inside the room and left.

Bolan locked the door and repeated his scan of the room. This time the device detected nothing, but he and Grimaldi did a thorough hands-on search just in case.

"Looks clean," Bolan said.

"It does," Grimaldi agreed. "Seems like somebody was expecting us," he said as he unzipped his suitcase. "Le Pierre, you think?"

Bolan shook his head. "Hard to say at this point, but I'm not sure our little buddy Le Pierre would have the means to set up that kind of sophisticated bugging equipment."

They unpacked quickly, knowing that Brognola had arranged a meeting somewhere on the island with the FBI agent.

Inside Bolan's case case were the slide, barrel, pin and recoil spring of Bolan's field-striped Beretta 93R, along with four fully loaded magazines. Next, he removed a supply of additional ammunition and a folded Espada knife, which he clipped to his belt so it was concealed inside his pants. Finally, he pulled out the upper and barrel portions of a SIG Sauer forty caliber P226 and handed it to Grimaldi.

Jack grinned wryly as he assembled the weapon. "Maybe I should've shown Capitaine Le Pierre that mine's bigger than his."

"Why crush the guy's already fragile ego?" Bolan said, putting together the Beretta. In a matter of seconds both men had their pistols fully assembled. Bolan checked the safety, inserted a magazine and racked back the slide to chamber a round. He then released the magazine and pressed another round in place, assuring a full load. As usual, two of the clips held standard ammunition, with jacketed ball and hollowpoints alternated, and the other two held special ammunition. One was marked with green to indicate frangible ammunition that was designed to avoid overpenetration, and the other contained armor-piercing rounds. Grimaldi sorted out a similar array of ammo and loaded his SIG, using the decocking lever to place it on safe.

Bolan then dug out two sets of sport-utility shoes that looked as if they had been made for mountain hiking. He passed a pair to Grimaldi, then twisted the metal cleats on one shoe and pulled the thick sole away. He took out a folded shoulder holster, looked at it and tossed it to the pilot.

"That one's yours," he said, and repeated the process with the second shoe. This one contained the shoulder rig for his Beretta. Grimaldi was taking apart the other pair, which contained small but powerful radios and ear mics.

"Hal did not disappoint," Grimaldi said, emitting a low whistle.

With weapons and gear assembled and ready for use, both men changed shirts and slipped their guns into their holsters, checking to make sure their new outfits fully concealed the pistols.

Bolan's handheld chimed with an incoming email. He picked it up and read it, then turned to Grimaldi. "It's from Hal. The meet with the FBI man is set. Fifteen minutes. Remember that mountain plateau we passed on the way from the airport?"

Grimaldi nodded.

Bolan gave himself one final check in the mirror to make sure the hang of his shirt properly covered up the Beretta. "You ready?"

"As they say—" Grimaldi smoothed out his sleeveless BDU shirt and grabbed his SIG Sauer "—I was born ready."

WILLARD FORSYTHE EVERETT III stood on the catwalk adjacent to the control room on the platform rig and watched as the helicopter made its landing on the helipad below. Edwin Grimes stood next to him, waiting like a bird dog eager for any sign of approval. Everett shot a quick glance at Grimes and began a mental assessment as to when it would be convenient to dump the man. He had proved useful, but lately his missteps, especially that fiasco with the yacht, had started to get under Everett's skin.

On the helipad, a squad of fifteen men made their way out of the bird as the rotors slowed to a stop. All of them were dressed in dark, camouflaged uniforms and wore matching helmets with night vision goggles attached.

"You're sure these guys are clear on the mission?" Everett asked. "I told you, we can't afford any slipups."

"Zelenkov assured me they're top-notch," Grimes responded. "Like I said, a couple are ex-Spetsnaz, just like him."

Everett pressed his lips together and watched the squad assembling below. Grimes seemed overly impressed by this Spetsnaz bullshit. If these Ruskies were so special, why had they been drummed out of the Russian army? He concentrated his gaze on the group of them, each one holding his AK-47 at port arms. Zelenkov, whose rifle was slung over his right shoulder, walked back and forth in front of the group, barking something in Russian loud enough for the words to drift up to the catwalk. Vince Tanner, Everett's assistant security chief, stood off to the side. He was clad in similar combat BDUs and was also armed with an AK-47. Zelenkov barked a command and the group snapped to attention.

"Anyone can look impressive doing D and C," Everett said. "Have they seen any combat?"

"All vets of the conflict in Chechnya," Grimes said.

"But do they know anything about ship assaults?"

"Zelenkov says they trained for it. Should be a cake-walk." Grimes gestured down at the group. "Besides, Tanner's going with them to keep us updated. What could go wrong?"

"There's always something that could go wrong." Everett watched the formation a few seconds more. "Tell Zelenkov I want to see him now. Before he leaves."

Grimes nodded.

"What about those new Americans that came in?" Everett asked. "You get them checked out?"

"Le Pierre rousted them on the way from the airport. Didn't find any weapons, which made them appear legit. Then they pulled a fast one at the hotel. Demanded to switch rooms. Smelled something funny, apparently, and the one guy threatened to puke."

Everett frowned. "Sounds like bullshit. They must have noticed the bugs. They're probably CIA or something. NSA at the very least."

"They're on the way to meet the FBI agent on the mountain plateau as we speak." The yelling had ceased from below and both men glanced downward. Zelenkov was looking up at them, and Grimes motioned for the Russian to come up to the control room area.

"What's that FBI agent's name again?" Everett asked Grimes.

"Tyler. Tim Tyler."

Everett smirked and thought for a moment. "If the U.S. government is sending more agents down, it's a given that they're sure Monk is here. Sooner or later they've got to figure I have him."

Grimes nodded.

Everett stroked the stubble around his upper lip, then traced the lines down to his chin. He liked the feel of it under his fingertips—a reassurance that he still had plenty of testosterone. "Le Pierre's man still with the corn husker?"

"Of course."

"Good," Everett said. "Tell him to stall the meeting a bit. Arrange a little reception party for them. Make it look like it's the work of Boudrous and his boys. Have them take out a couple of bystanders, too, for good measure. Zelenkov can send one of his goons to supervise it just in case."

Grimes's brow furrowed, as if he didn't think hitting the Feds at this juncture was such a good idea. Everett reconsidered the decision. Tipping their hand this early could bring more heat from Washington, and if things went wrong, more agents would be flying down here, perhaps upsetting his timeline. But Everett decided it would work, and this weasel's critical expression bothered him. "You got something you want to say about that?"

"No, sir," Grimes said.

"I didn't think so." Everett thought about how much he'd like to get Grimes in the ring and beat the shit out of him, just on general principle. He put it on his list of things to do, and smiled. "As I said before, this little mishap will be something for the French and the Dutch to deal with. Why do you think I arranged for Boudrous to come back from Haiti? He's the perfect fall guy for any disasters that might beset some American agents. A good chess player is always thinking at least two moves ahead." Everett smacked his right fist into the palm of his left hand. "Regardless, this weak sister we have in the White House now won't dare do anything until he rehashes all his options. Hell, it might even be beneficial to our big plan. Sow the seeds of public outrage and discontent over the tragic deaths of some more Americans. Get people fired up. Then, when the big bang goes off, the President won't have any choice but to act." He let his voice trail off as he looked wistfully at the horizon. "It'll be a new dawn for the United States of America."

"It sure will, boss."

Everett frowned again. Grimes's ass-kissing sickened him. The weasel was obviously trying to sound convincing, but he was still a little weasel. But they'd been on a one-way track ever since they'd found that Russian sub, and Everett knew he had to finish the game with the players he had. No substitutions, no turning back.

Zelenkov's heavy, muscular frame sounded like a jackhammer as he ran up the metal stairs to the catwalk. At the top, he whipped a salute at Everett, who returned it. The guy wasn't even breathing hard.

"You have someone back on the island who can lead an ambush assault on some Americans with a group of Boudrous's men?" Everett asked. "In a hurry?"

Zelenkov thought for a moment and then nodded. His gray eyes didn't show emotion. He tilted his head back and the blue-and-black tattoos on his neck seemed to roll upward as the thick muscles shifted. "I do have such a man," he said, taking out his cell phone.

"Good," Everett said. "They'll be on the mountain plateau in about twenty minutes. Three Americans, with an island policeman. Make it look like the work of a band of thugs."

Zelenkov nodded as he spoke in Russian into his cell. "I will need a few more details," he added to Everett in English.

Everett turned to Grimes and motioned with his head. "Get with him on this. Make sure it's hard and clean."

"Will do, boss." His smile looked forced. "We'll take care of it."

They'd better, Everett thought. I don't have time for fuck-ups or fools.

**4**

Bolan and Grimaldi leaned against the three-foot-high cement wall that overlooked the lush vegetation of the valley below. Beyond the trees, they could see the coastline and ocean. The plateau was the perfect place to snap some pictures of the gorgeous island scenery. As the road wound along the next bend, the view would expand to include the ramshackle village that preceded the strip of luxury hotels. This lookout appeared to have been bulldozed flat as the road was cut through the mountains. At one time, perhaps, it had been a peak of some sort. Now it was forty yards of blacktop adjacent to the two-lane road, with several parking spaces and an array of picnic tables in the center. Bolan and Grimaldi's rental sat in one of the spots nearby, while another Citroën was parked at the opposite end. A young couple, probably in their mid-twenties, took turns posing for photos in front of the scenic background.

Grimaldi drummed his fingers impatiently on the cement. "You think he forgot about us?"

Bolan glanced at his watch. The FBI man was fifteen minutes late. "Hal said it was all set up."

Grimaldi puffed up his cheeks and exhaled. "What's this dude's name again?"

"Tim Tyler."

"Wasn't there an old comic strip with that name, or something?"

"Yeah. *Tim Tyler's Luck*."

Grimaldi snorted. "Well, I hope this Fed had some *luck* getting a line on that Monk guy. I'm starting to get an uneasy feeling about this one."

"You and me both," Bolan said. He heard the sound of a car approaching and looked toward the far curve. A white police jeep crested the hill and began veering toward them. The driver wore the crisp blue-and-white island police uniform. The man in the passenger seat was dressed in a blue suit, white shirt and necktie. He looked young, maybe twenty-five, and had short cropped red hair and a spray of freckles across his face.

"Will you look at that?" Grimaldi said. "A beautiful, seventy-nine degree Caribbean afternoon and this guy's dressed like Opie Taylor in a three-piece suit."

The jeep pulled in next to their Citroën and stopped. The vehicle had no doors and the canvas roof was pulled back. The young guy unbuckled his seat belt, hopped out and walked toward them, holding out his open palm.

"I'm Special Agent Tyler from the Bureau," he said. "Sorry we're so late. Are you Cooper?" Tyler's face was almost boyish.

"I am," he said, shaking Tyler's hand. He introduced Grimaldi, who also shook hands with the agent.

"This is Corporal Gaston of the island police," Tyler said, pointing to the jeep's driver. "They assigned him to help me check out the hotels and other spots on both sides of the island. He speaks French, English and Dutch."

"What? No Italian?" Grimaldi shook Gaston's hand.

Bolan shook the corporal's hand in turn, noticing that it was damp.

"How do you do?" Gaston asked. He smiled, but his

dark face was shiny with sweat, too. "You no doubt have much to discuss in private. I will leave you to your privacy."

He walked over to the picnic tables, taking out his cell phone as he went. Beyond him, the young couple still flirted playfully, posing for the camera.

"So you two are with the Justice Department?" Tyler asked.

"We are," Bolan said.

"No offense, but this is a Bureau case." Tyler's face scrunched up. "Why did they send you two to investigate?"

"Maybe they figured you could use some backup," Bolan said. "You down here by yourself?"

"Yeah." Tyler clicked his tongue. "For the moment, anyway. The agents I was originally paired with got pulled to help check things out in Puerto Rico. The vice president's going to be there the day after tomorrow to attend the International Caribbean Security Conference."

"We heard about that," Bolan said.

Tyler nodded. "Well, anyway, so far we haven't been able to trace Monk since he was in San Juan. That's the last recorded place he was at."

"What about his daughter?"

"She got here about a week ago, but checked out of her hotel room and hasn't been seen since. Allegedly said she was going to spend some time on a friend's boat. So at the moment, we don't know if either of them is on this island. There's no official record of Monk going through customs here, either."

"Did you get our tip about that shady customs agent?" Bolan asked.

"Van der Hyden?"

Bolan nodded.

"Yeah, in fact, we just got back from the airport. We

checked the man's station and locker and found a substantial amount of cash."

"I'm not surprised," Bolan said. "Did you ask him if Monk came through on a false passport?"

"Yep," Tyler said.

"Well, what did he say?" Grimaldi asked.

Tyler scratched his head again. "Not much. After we took him off the floor and started questioning him, he clammed up. Immediately asked for a lawyer. I had no choice but to turn him over to the Dutch authorities. He'll most likely lose his job and be sent back to the Netherlands to face possible charges of official malfeasance."

Grimaldi frowned and shook his head. "I wish you would've waited till we got there. We might have been able to get something out of the guy."

"Now, now," Tyler said, waggling his index finger in front of Grimaldi's face. "Remember, we're here on the sovereign territory of another country. Actually, in this case two separate countries, which complicates matters even more. We have to make sure our behavior stays within the appropriate confines of international law and go through proper, diplomatic channels."

Bolan was watching Gaston. His head was jerking back and forth as he spoke on his cell phone. He cast a nervous glance in their direction and resumed talking. The hairs on the back of Bolan's neck began to rise and he made out the high-pitched whine of an engine approaching. He asked Tyler if he had a weapon.

"I do," the agent said, patting his chest.

"Better get ready," Bolan said. "I think you're going to have to use it."

A dirty gray pickup truck whipped around the corner. The bed was filled with rough-looking men. The one in the passenger seat turned his pale, shaved head and yelled something at the driver, who angled right for the plateau's parking area. Two of the men in the back of the truck straightened up and leveled AK-47s over the cab.

"Take cover!" Bolan yelled. "Jack, I'm going for those tourists."

"Roger that, Cooper."

Bolan reached under his shirt and pulled out the Beretta 93R as he zigzagged through the picnic tables. "Get down!" he shouted at the couple.

They turned and looked at him, fear fixed on both their faces. Bolan ran past Gaston, who was now standing with his arms stretched over his head. He hadn't even touched the Manurhin MR 73 revolver holstered on his right side.

Bolan was about three steps away from the couple when the first rifle rounds zipped by him, with an accompanying burst of automatic fire. He crouched and dived into the man, reaching out and grabbing the woman and pulling her down, as well.

"*Qu'est-ce que c'est?*" the man asked.

Bolan motioned with his left hand for them to stay down, and whirled to face their adversaries. He flipped the select lever on the Beretta to the three-dot position— 3-round bursts—grabbed the bench of the closest picnic table and flipped it onto its side.

Grimaldi and Tyler had taken cover behind the Citroën and were returning fire. Bolan counted eight men total from the truck, spread out across the plateau. Some crouched next to the tailgate of their vehicle, some stood in the bed leaning over the cab, and two others stood out in the open as they fired their Kalashnikovs on full-auto.

Bolan took those two out first. He snapped the front handle down for better control and sent a 3-round burst into each of them. They curled and fell forward. Grimaldi picked off one of the rooftop shooters. The other one ducked down. The big bald guy, shouting orders in what sounded like Russian, held his AK-47 up over the fender and sent a barrage at Grimaldi and Tyler, then aimed the barrel at Bolan. The picnic table's thick boards deflected the rounds as they pierced the wood. Bolan glanced back at the tourists, who were still on the ground behind him, sheer terror on their faces. If they stayed there, hopefully, they wouldn't get hit. He fired another 3-round burst toward the big Russian guy just as Gaston ran past him, as fast as he could, away from the fight. Bolan swore at the retreating cop, but as he did so, the back of the corporal's crisp blue shirt was perforated by a track of bullet holes. Gaston took two more steps, slowed and fell on his face.

Bolan saw the Russian guy smiling as he looked up over the top of his rifle.

The soldier dashed forward, shooting a burst as he ran, then dived between the legs of another picnic table. He continued to roll as more rounds zipped around him. When he stopped, his arms were extended in ready position and he had a clear shot at the Russian.

The bald man's face reflected surprise, then a grimace as he spotted Bolan. The Russian swiveled the barrel of his rifle toward him, but the soldier had already acquired a sight picture and sent 3-rounds into the man's side. He lurched back, his rifle still pointed in Bolan's direction. Bolan fired another burst, this time elevating his aim. The Russian's head jerked and he recoiled backward, a cloud of scarlet mist exploding from his right temple. As the man crumpled to the asphalt, the Executioner was up and running.

Bolan knew from experience the best way to deal with an ambush was to fight your way out, and he fired more 3-round bursts as he ran. Out of the corner of his eye he saw Grimaldi rising and firing his SIG at the shooters in the truck. Two more fell. The remaining two adversaries were crouching by the side of the truck, screaming at each other. It was clear they were panicking, and Bolan ran at an angle to outflank them. He knew that Grimaldi would be doing the same.

One of the men saw Bolan and raised his rifle. The Executioner dived into a slide, and as his left side hit the hard asphalt, he brought the Beretta in front of him and sent two bursts along the ground. The rounds zipped under the carriage of the pickup and into the feet and legs of the last two shooters. He saw them dancing in pain as Grimaldi rounded the other side. Jack took out the one closest to him and Bolan shot the other man in the chest. Both fell to the ground, their AK-47s tumbling out of their hands.

Bolan kept moving, keeping his Beretta trained on the fallen adversaries. He and Grimaldi kicked the rifles away from the bodies as they checked them. When they had determined that each man was, in fact, dead, Bolan straightened up and flipped his Beretta to Safe.

Tyler ran over to them, panting and still holding his pistol. The slide was locked back, indicating he'd fired all the rounds in his magazine.

"Is it over?" the FBI man asked. His voice sounded faraway, distorted.

"Looks like it." The ringing had started to fade from Bolan's ears. Grimaldi walked over to them and pointed to Tyler's gun.

"Looks like you're out of ammo," he said.

Bolan stooped and removed a pistol from the big bald guy's belt. It was a Russian Tokarev 9 mm.

"I've never been in anything like that before," Tyler admitted. "You two guys are unbelievable."

"First shootout?" Bolan asked.

The agent nodded, his face pinched.

Bolan turned and went to check on the young couple. He found them right where he had left them, lying prone on the ground in back of the overturned picnic table. He stooped down and gently placed a hand on the man's shoulder. His head shot up, terror still etched across his face. Bolan smiled. "The worst is over," he said, gesturing toward the young woman. "Are you both okay?"

She looked up, her face streaked with tears. "We are not harmed," she said.

Bolan gave them a reassuring nod and did a quick assessment of the situation. He went over to examine the fallen island policeman. The man was dead, his weapon still in its holster. A cell phone lay in pieces next to his outstretched hand. Bolan would have liked to have been able to check the last call the dead man had made, or maybe scroll through his contacts, but he already had a pretty good idea who Gaston had phoned. The timing of this ambush had been a little too coincidental.

In the distance Bolan heard the wail of a siren. Sounds like the cavalry's coming, he thought. Late, as usual.

**5**

Everett watched the television monitor intently in the platform rig's control room. Next to him, Andrei Rinzihov, an older man with sparse gray hair and thick-framed, circular glasses, gazed at the screen, as well. Grimes stood behind them. The camera showed the first submersible's mechanical arm reach into the square hole in the side of the submarine and pull away another piece of metal debris. The divers, specially outfitted in heavy-duty wasp suits, stood by with their welding tools. The arm of the second submersible hovered above them.

"What the hell are they waiting for?" Everett asked. "They've been working on that damn thing for days."

Grimes turned to the technician manning the control panel. "Find out what's up down there?"

The tech nodded and spoke into his microphone, asking the dive team leader for a progress report.

"Checking the radiation levels again," he replied.

"I thought they just did that," Everett said. "Tell them to speed it up. We're on a timetable here."

The tech relayed Everett's message to the team.

"Roger that, base," the team leader said. "We're moving as fast as we can."

Everett's face darkened. "Tell him it's not fast enough."

Again the tech relayed the information.

"We've been at this around the clock," the diver answered in a weary voice. "You think you can do better, come on down."

Everett felt a growing rage. "That son of a bitch is asking to get fired. Tell him I'm the one calling the shots up here."

The tech looked nervous. "Be advised, team leader," he said into the microphone, "that the boss is topside in the control room."

Silence, then, "Sorry, sir. But we have to make sure the area's safe to enter."

*Safe*? Everett thought, still feeling the burn of anger. I don't have *time* for safe.

GRIMES WATCHED AS the flush slowly began to dissipate from his boss's face. The dive team leader no doubt knew he'd be disciplined regardless of the apology. Being fired wouldn't be his biggest fear, either. Not with Everett's top-secret plan in the works. If Everett wanted to let the man go, it would be with a gunshot, not a pink slip. No wonder the diver was so contrite.

That was one way to inspire loyalty. Grimes smirked.

Rinzihov laughed softly and placed his palm on Everett's shoulder. "Willard, my friend, you must learn the value of patience." His words were laced with a heavy Russian accent. "They must proceed with caution and prudence. The cameras have already verified that there is at least one intact RU-100 Veter inside. Why do we not engage in a game of chess and let your men do their work?"

That would be a godsend, thought Grimes. Rinzihov squeezed Everett's shoulder. The boss made everyone on the platform nervous with his constant scrutiny and temper tantrums. If Rinzihov could get him away from the control booth and into a game of chess for a while, it would go a long way toward making this delicate part of the recovery run smoother.

The old Russian had been an expert in the now-defunct Soviet nuclear program. Everett had recruited him after the end of his involvement with Iran's nuclear research program. He was one of the lucky ones. The other five Russian nuclear scientists that had been "assisting" Iran had been killed in a mysterious plane crash a few years ago. At the time, Rinzihov had been in Canada trying to promote his diamond business. The Russian scientist was smart enough to know the crash had been no accident, and promptly accepted Everett's offer to go underground in hopes of furthering his diamond project.

That project was eventually abandoned, however, when Everett's drilling survey crew found something far more interesting: a sunken Soviet Oscar class submarine resting on the ocean floor in the Caribbean. It was, as Everett called it, a message from God. And the plot to begin the deadly salvage and the subsequent "Operation Big Boom" had begun. Now, they'd finally cut through both hulls of the submarine, removed the thick rubber cushioning in between, and reached the crucial point: entry into the missile compartment. So far, everything was holding firm—radiation levels stable, no shifting of the wreckage on the seabed, no breach detected in the reactor compartment, and two SS-N-16 Stallion missiles with attached atomic warheads—everything Everett needed to change the world.

"We're too close for me to concentrate on chess," Everett said. He refocused his gaze on the screen. "What are they doing now?"

"Getting ready to remove the first missile from the compartment, sir," the technician said.

Grimes noticed the tech was sweating so heavily that the armpits and back of his blue uniform shirt were sodden.

"We don't need the whole missile," Everett said. "Just the warhead."

Rinzihov laughed again. "It is far easier to grab hold of the bigger fish at three thousand meters than only the top. If the top were to slip from their grasp it would be like combing the bottom for a lost seashell."

"Everybody shut the hell up," Everett bellowed. He leaned over the tech's shoulder, his face only a foot from the screen, and watched intently. "Get me a damn status report from down there."

The tech radioed the submersible for an update.

"We've secured the target." The voice sounded tense as it came through the speaker. "Beginning removal process at this time."

Everyone stood transfixed. Finally, the tech managed to say, "Roger," into the microphone.

Bubbles floated up from the side of the wreckage. No movement. No sound. The scene seemed frozen in the greenish glow of the underwater lighting. Finally, the mechanical arm turned and began to pull back. A long, cone-like tip began to emerge from the hole.

"Andrei," Everett said, his voice hushed, breathless, "is that it?"

The old Russian leaned over, patted Everett's shoulder twice and said in a reassuring voice, "Indeed, my friend, it is."

THE THREE POLICE jeeps rolled up, sirens still wailing, as Bolan was getting out of the shot-up Citroën. The first two jeeps contained four officers each, and the last one was driven by Sergeant Gipardieu, with Captain Le Pierre in the passenger seat. The squad of island policemen jumped out of the vehicles brandishing pump action shotguns, and proceeded to point them at Bolan, Grimaldi and Tyler. Bolan's hands were empty so he raised them above his head. Grimaldi holstered his SIG Sauer and did the same. Tyler, however, still seemed to be in shock. He stood there holding his weapon with the slide still locked back.

"Better drop your gun," Grimaldi said. "I don't think they realize we're the good guys."

Tyler blinked twice, looked at the pistol and then let it fall to the ground. He, too, raised his hands.

Sergeant Gipardieu marched toward them, a refrigerator on legs, and barked orders in French to the policemen holding the shotguns. Captain Le Pierre slowly got out of the jeep and sauntered forward, his hands clasped behind his back like a prince surveying a formation of the royal guards.

"Hey, Capitaine Le Pierre," Grimaldi called out. "How about calling off your boys so we can lower our hands?"

The officer ignored the request, but scrutinized each of them as he walked by. Bodies and brass casings littered the ground and crunched under Le Pierre's shiny shoes. He went to the young couple, who were still cowering on the other side of the plateau.

Tyler called out to him, "Captain Le Pierre, it's Special Agent Tyler from the FBI."

If he heard, Le Pierre gave no indication. He kept his leisurely pace as he approached the tourists.

"You know," Grimaldi said, "I don't think he likes us for some reason."

"Just relax," Bolan said. "After getting through that firefight, we don't want to get shot at this juncture."

They held their stances, hands elevated, for a good five minutes while Le Pierre engaged in a long conversation with the young couple. Occasionally, he turned his head toward the three of them. Finally, he shook hands with the two young people, then turned and came back to Bolan,

Grimaldi and Tyler. When he was about ten feet away he said something in French to Gipardieu, who in turn bellowed an order for the island policemen to lower their shotguns. Le Pierre strolled up to the FBI man.

"Agent Tyler," he said, "my apologies for not responding to you sooner. Can you tell me what has occurred here?"

Tyler compressed his lips, held the expression, then said, "Isn't that obvious, Captain? We were attacked by some gunmen."

Le Pierre lifted his eyebrow again as he glanced around. "That is obvious. And how did this come to be?"

Tyler looked frustrated and about to snap. Not wanting to deal with a confrontation, Bolan stepped forward. "Captain, I think if you take a look at that body over there you may get some answers."

Le Pierre turned toward him with a crisp pivot. "Oh? And how do you know this?"

Bolan held up his hands, palms outward as he walked to the corpse of the Russian man. He moved with slow deliberation. When he got to the body, he squatted and pulled up the dead man's sleeve, revealing an intricate latticework of blue-and-black ink. Le Pierre showed no reaction.

"This guy's probably associated with the Russian *Mafya*," Bolan said.

"Yeah," Grimaldi said, "you don't get tats like that at the local tattoo parlor."

Le Pierre shook his head. "No, these men are obviously island thugs. They work for a master criminal named Boudrous. I shall have him brought in for questioning."

"Round up the usual suspects, huh?" Grimaldi asked.

Le Pierre's eyes flashed at him, then back to Bolan. "And who are you really, Monsieur Cooper? I strongly doubt that journalists would be carrying the weapons you used here." He paused, then issued a command in French.

The policemen raised their shotguns once again. "That reminds me. You will all surrender your weapons at this time."

"Weapons?" Grimaldi said with a smirk. "What makes you think we have weapons?"

"Do not play games," Le Pierre said. "I am not in the mood. Those two people told me you have sophisticated weapons," he said, gesturing at the tourists. "You will surrender them *now*."

"Yeah, well, maybe they didn't see things too clearly," Grimaldi said, crossing his arms. "Considering they were cowering on the pavement the whole time."

Le Pierre smiled again and snapped his fingers. "Sergeant Gipardieu. Search them."

"What?" Grimaldi said. "You can't do that."

Le Pierre's thin mustache lifted on the left side of his mouth. "Do you wish me to advise you of our rights?"

"Jack," Bolan said, "stand down. We've got to pick our battles, and this isn't one of them."

"Excellent advice, *monsieur*," Le Pierre said. "I suggest you both obey it."

Grimaldi frowned and raised his hands above his head. "Go ahead, then."

Bolan raised his arms, too.

Gipardieu patted down Grimaldi and ripped the SIG Sauer out of his shoulder holster. The sergeant turned to Bolan, whose open garment revealed his shoulder rig. Gipardieu grabbed the butt of the pistol sticking out of holster and pulled it out, staring at the Russian Tokarev 9 mm.

"This is your weapon?" Le Pierre asked, his eyebrows rising skeptically.

"I hope you realize that if we didn't have some firepower these assholes would have wiped us off the map," Grimaldi said.

"That is not my concern," Le Pierre said. "You have violated French law. And may I remind you that I lost one of my men in this fracas?"

"Corporal Gaston's death was unfortunate," Bolan said. "Any idea how these guys might have known we were meeting your man and Agent Tyler up here?"

"I told you. Boudrous. The man has ears all over the island." The captain muttered something to Gipardieu and the sergeant stuck Grimaldi's SIG and the Tokarev into the leather belt surrounding his ample middle.

"Captain," Tyler said, stepping forward. "I must formally protest. These men are members of an official government agency of the United States."

"That must be verified through proper channels." Le Pierre smiled benignly. "But you will be able to keep your weapon, out of professional courtesy, of course."

"This is outrageous," Tyler said. "I'm going to—"

"Tim," Bolan said, "let's split the difference and let the State Department work things out." He turned to Le Pierre. "Do you need us to make a formal statement right now?"

Le Pierre stood silently for a moment, his eyes narrowing. "That will not be necessary at this time. However, you must come by my office in the morning. As I said, this is obviously the work of one of our local bandits, Arsen Boudrous. An illegal Haitian. We will assemble a force and begin a search." He barked some commands and the island cops began collecting all the fallen weapons from the dead as they worked their way back to their jeeps. Two of them went to retrieve their fallen compatriot.

Grimaldi's jaw dropped. "You're not going to process this crime scene?"

"I will leave two of my men here to guard it, and send

another contingent to have this area cleaned up," Le Pierre said. He began heading back toward his vehicle. Gipardieu glared at Bolan and Grimaldi, then gestured to the young couple and turned to follow his captain. The two tourists stood shakily and slid into the backseat of Le Pierre's jeep. Their Citroën would clearly not be moving anytime soon.

"Hey, what about us?" Grimaldi called. "The tires on our car are all shot to hell."

"Then I suggest you begin walking, if you so wish," Le Pierre said over his shoulder. "I will send a taxi for you when I get back to headquarters."

"How about a receipt for my SIG?" Grimaldi yelled.

Le Pierre settled himself into the seat and lifted his lip in a sneer. "*Sans discussion.* Come by my office in the morning." He made a sharp gesture and Gipardieu shoved the jeep into gear and roared away. The other cars followed, each pair of eyes shooting daggers at them as they passed.

The two remaining island policemen walked to the edge of the plateau, leaned their shotguns against the concrete barrier and began smoking cigarettes.

Tyler's face sagged into an anxious frown. "I don't know what to say about all this." He tried to holster his pistol, realized the slide was still locked back, then fumbled as he tried to release it. Grimaldi took the weapon from him and freed the magazine.

"You got another mag?" he asked.

Tyler nodded and reached into his pants pocket. He gave the magazine to the pilot, who inserted it and hit the slide release, chambering a round. He pressed the decocking lever to make the weapon safe, and handed it back to the FBI man. Then he turned to Bolan. "What now?"

Before the soldier could answer, he heard the high, whining sound of an engine, and the three men glanced toward the bend in the road. Bolan ran to the Citroën, pulled open the door and reached into the backseat. Seconds later he emerged with his Beretta 93R.

Bolan held the weapon down by his leg as a sporty Jaguar roared around the curve and sped toward them. The two policemen stayed where they were, placidly watching the sports car but taking no action to try to stop it. The vehicle swerved around the litter of bodies on the plateau and came to a stop in front of Bolan, Grimaldi and Tyler. The driver was an exquisitely beautiful woman in her mid-thirties with a mane of blond hair. Her green eyes surveyed the scene, taking in the corpses and finally centering on the dead Russian.

"What happened here?" she asked in French.

"Do you speak English?" Bolan asked in her language. "So my friends can understand."

She smiled. "Ah, Americans, I take it? And, it appears, very busy ones." She gestured at the carnage.

"Traffic accident," Grimaldi said. "Real bad one."

"A pity." The woman canted her head and looked at him, then back to Bolan. "And your car is disabled, as well. Perhaps I could give one of you a ride back to your hotel."

Bolan turned to Grimaldi, his back to the woman. "I'll go with her and organize a ride for you two. You stay with Tyler and keep an eye on these cops," he whispered, subtly shoving the Beretta into his belt.

Grimaldi glanced over at the police officers, who still seemed uninterested in anything but their smokes. Bolan turned, opened the door of Jaguar and slid into the passenger seat. "This is very kind of you, miss. Name's Matt Cooper."

# 6

She was wearing blue shorts and a sleeveless white blouse. Cool attire for an equally cool lady, Bolan thought as he watched her right hand glide the gearshift through the six positions until she leveled it out at about sixty miles per hour on the straightaway portions of the road. The sharp bends required constant downshifting, which she also handled with the aplomb of a professional driver. Bolan glanced appreciatively at her muscular legs as they worked the clutch and gas pedals.

"What part of Russia are you from?" Bolan asked.

"And how did you know I was Russian?"

"Your lovely accent."

She flashed a devilish smile, displaying perfect white teeth, except for a gold crown next to the right incisor. "Am I making you nervous, Mr. Cooper?"

Bolan remembered the old Soviet Union stainless steel crowns and figured her to be from the new generation of recruits. The Russians knew how to attract excellent candidates at a very young age. "Not at all," he said. "I love to fly."

She tossed her head back and laughed, then downshifted again as they went around another hairpin curve. "So are you going to tell me what brings you to this lovely little island?"

"Me? I'm a journalist, covering the big movie being filmed down here. How about you?"

"Vacation, of course," she said. "Every Russian girl dreams of one day going to the Caribbean, especially after a cold Moscow winter."

"This island in particular seems quite popular with your countrymen," he said.

"Perhaps." Her lips formed a sly smile. "I would not know. I am here with a friend."

They rounded the final turn and the roadway leveled off as the line of beachfront hotels appeared, perhaps a half mile away. She accelerated and shifted back into sixth gear.

"Was that big, bald-headed dead guy back on the plateau one of your friends?" Bolan asked.

She made a tsk-tsking sound and shook her finger in his direction. "You should know better, Mr. Cooper." She tilted her head again, giving him a long, appraising stare. "Have we met before, Mr. Cooper?"

Bolan smiled. "You must have me mixed up with someone else. My evil twin brother, maybe. But since I've introduced myself…"

"My name is Natalia Valencia Kournikova." Without asking which hotel he was staying at, she drove down the main thoroughfare and pulled up in front of the Omni. She stopped the Jaguar and glanced at Bolan with her piercing eyes. "How is this?"

"You're a good guesser," Bolan said. "This is the right hotel."

"A coincidence," she said. "I am staying at this hotel myself."

Bolan started to get out of the car. "A coincidence indeed. Thanks for the lift. Or should I say *spasibo*?"

"You're welcome," she said, holding out a card. "As we said, maybe we will meet again."

"Another time, then," Bolan said, taking it. "And hopefully, another place."

He closed the car door and watched as she pulled out of the drive and zoomed back onto the thoroughfare. The card had Cyrillic lettering on the front, and 1204 and a phone number written on the back. Bolan didn't believe for a second that this woman was on the island to soak up the sun. She was obviously working for Russian intelligence. The question was whether she was GRU, SVR, or FSB.

"WHAT THE HELL do you mean, *it didn't go well?* That's putting it mildly." Everett slammed his fist onto the polished wood coffee table. "It sounds like a goddamn clusterfuck."

Grimes said nothing, glad that most of the walls in Everett's plush, inland mansion were virtually soundproof. Not that anyone other than the guards and a few "guests" were around to hear, anyway. He had expected the boss's rant to be loud after he learned about the botched ambush. Grimes also knew better than to point out that it had been Everett's decision to send one of Zelenkov's men to supervise Boudrous's ragtag bunch of thugs. But then again, they should have been able to do it with ease. The only one who was supposed to have had a weapon was that FBI bozo, Tyler, and he didn't look that formidable at all.

Everett must have read his thoughts.

"I thought Le Pierre told us those new Americans didn't have any weapons?"

"He did," Grimes said. "Obviously, they were a bit tougher than we anticipated."

"We should've acted as soon as we knew they'd found those damn bugs." Everett swore and slammed his fist on the table again. This time the blow was so hard it sent a series of cracks across the finely polished surface. "Where do we stand on the *Xerxes?*"

"That's the good news. Tanner reported that it went like clockwork. Zelenkov and his men boarded the ship under the cover of darkness and executed a quick, hostile take-over. Not a shot was fired." Grimes tried a slight smile. "Like he said, they're pros."

"Too bad the one he sent to the ambush wasn't." Everett ran his index finger and thumb over the stubble around his upper lip. "What about the captain and crew?"

"All in custody."

"How many are there?" Everett asked.

"Forty-eight total. Other than a skeleton crew, kept under guard to run the ship, the rest are locked up. What do you want Tanner to do with them?"

Everett considered this for a moment. "He's got the video camera, right? He and Zelenkov can make the captain and a few crew members record some martyr videos. Zelenkov speaks Farsi. Hold the disks so we can send them to Al Jazeera once the shit hits the fan."

Grimes nodded. "What about the rest of the crew?"

"Tell Tanner to keep them locked up for now, except for the ones he needs to keep the ship on course." Everett's fingers traced over his upper lip again. "I don't want to take the chance on somebody finding any bodies floating around. When we get ready for the final preparation, we can dispose of them."

Disposables, Grimes thought. Good.

"The Coast Guard's probably still out in force looking for that damn yacht," Everett said.

Ah, yes, the yacht. More collateral damage.

The boss stroked his chin. "You said we also had some Russian arrivals?"

"Yeah," Grimes said. "A man and a woman. Supposed to be tourists."

"Tourists my ass. They're Russian FSB or GRU. Probably got wind that Rinzihov was here." He frowned. "We're getting more foreign agents on this goddamn island than we are illegal aliens."

"Do you want me to arrange another reception party for them and the Americans?"

"After the last debacle?" Everett walked to the large picture window that overlooked the valley leading to the bay. It was dark now and the lights from the harbor and restaurants that dotted the coast twinkled like stars. He stood there, arms at his sides, for a good thirty seconds. When he turned he had a smile on his face.

"Remember the first Gulf War?" he asked.

Grimes nodded.

"People criticized Bush for not going into Baghdad and getting rid of Saddam when he had the chance," Everett said. "But if he had, he would have lost the coalition that he had to kick that bastard out of Kuwait."

Grimes nodded again, knowing it was time for another of the boss's warped history lessons.

"But what the critics didn't have any concept of," Everett continued, "was how difficult it is to keep all the balls in the air at the same time."

Grimes knew where this was heading because he'd heard it so many times before.

"I'm confronted with a similar situation now, juggling all these different balls," Everett continued. "But this is another chess game entirely. This operation calls for precision timing of simultaneous events." He paused and raised his hands in front of him, interlocking his fingers. "Hell, it's like one of those *Star Trek* multilevel chessboards. But once everything is in place, it'll be a catalyst to the dawning of a new day. This current pretender in the White House will have no choice but to launch a full-scale, retaliatory nuclear attack against those damn Iranians. And once that happens, the rest of my plan will unfold like clockwork. The price of my oil holdings will skyrocket, and with the new fracking projects I've started this past year, we'll be out-producing the Saudis soon. And I'll be calling the shots. I won't even need to be president."

Grimes knew from experience that the boss had reached the end of his diatribe, but he still hadn't made a decision about the Russian and American agents. Grimes swallowed and waited a few more beats before asking again. "So, what do you want to do about the recent arrivals?"

Everett unlaced his fingers and regarded Grimes with disdain. Obviously, he felt that the dramatic effect of his lecture had gone south. "Don't do anything about them," he said, his voice harsh. He took a couple breaths. "There's an old adage—keep your friends close and your enemies closer. Just keep an eye on them for now. Hell, invite them all to the Mr. Galaxy party."

"Of course," Grimes said. He needed to get the hell out of here and toss down a drink or two. He was growing weary of playing the gofer for this rich madman, but he had no choice. He was in for the duration now, had to hold on for the ultimate payoff. Ending up being the right-hand man for one of the wealthiest, most powerful men on the planet was worth a few little inconveniences. Besides, pulling out now would be suicide, tantamount to betrayal in Everett's eyes, and the boss had one response for betrayal: death. "I'll see to it, sir," Grimes said.

"You do that," Everett responded, his lips still twisted into that strange smile of his. "And bring me Rinzihov and Monk. I want them to start working on breaking those safeguard codes on the fuses we've recovered. Like I said, we're on a special timetable here."

"Right away, boss." Grimes turned to go.

"Hold on," Everett said. "Get me a drink first. I need

one." He turned and gazed out the big window again, clasping his hands behind his back.

Just like a picture of Napoleon surveying one of his battlefields, Grimes thought as he went over to the wet bar. And he knew what had happened to Napoleon at Waterloo. But Napoleon never had a nuclear warhead at his disposal.

BOLAN PARKED HIS newly rented Citroën next to the shot-up rental on the plateau. He glanced over at the two island policemen, who showed little interest in his arrival. They continued to loll against the barrier, smoking cigarettes, and didn't so much as wave as Tyler and Grimaldi climbed into the car. Taking one last look at the grisly scene, Bolan pulled back onto the mountain road.

After dropping Tyler off at his hotel, the soldier parked on a side street so they could call Brognola for a sitrep. Grimaldi held up his cell phone. "I got a picture of that dead Russian's face and some of his tattoos. Figure maybe Aaron can run it through Interpol and maybe get an ID."

"Good thinking," Bolan said, taking out his satellite phone and dialing Brognola's number. The big Fed answered with a gruff "What's up?"

Bolan gave him a quick update, letting him know they were on their way back to the Omni.

"Roger that," Brognola said. "We'll work on getting you some more weapons by tomorrow. You need anything else?"

"Yeah. Jack's emailing you the picture of a dead guy. Looks to be Russian mafia. Any chance you can get us an ID?"

"A Russian? What the hell was he doing down there?"

"Unknown," Bolan said, "but I've heard it's every Russian's dream to come to the Caribbean on vacation."

Brognola laughed. "Yeah, the snow's probably beginning to melt in Moscow."

"Our dead guy isn't the only Russian down here. I got a ride back to my hotel from a woman, probably GRU or SVR. Gave me the name Natalia Valencia Kournikova."

"I'll check that out, too," Brognola said. "By the way, that yacht I told you about was found. All aboard are missing. Substantial amount of bullet holes and blood, too."

"Sounds like a hijacking. That ought to be enough to get some Coast Guard or Navy patrols in this area, right?"

"As much as we can, but the vessel was recovered quite a ways from the island, so there's nothing to directly link it to St. Francis except the original course they had charted."

"Maybe it's time for us to do a little sailing of our own. Thanks, Hal." Bolan ended the call. "Good news," he said to Grimaldi. "Hal's going to have another SIG sent over to you."

"I still plan to get the other one back from the cops," Grimaldi said. "What else?"

"They recovered the *Slice of Heaven*, that luxury yacht that went missing. Looks like it wasn't a pleasure cruise."

"That the hijacking you were talking about?"

Bolan nodded.

"So we're going fishing?" Grimaldi asked.

"In a manner of speaking. But let's think about what we've got so far." He held up his hand and ticked a point off on each finger. "A missing DOD analyst and his errant daughter, whom no one has seen. A recovered luxury yacht full of blood and bullet holes, but no bodies. A crooked Dutch customs agent, at least one equally crooked French cop, a dead Russian *Mafya* thug, more dead island flunkies, and a bunch of listening devices in our hotel room.

"And don't forget about the Russian babe in the Jag,"

Bolan added. "It all has to tie together somehow," the pilot said. "We've just got to find the common denominator."

"I think we already have," Bolan stated.

Grimaldi looked at him and cocked his head. "What?"

"Not what," he answered. "Who. There's only one man down here who has the clout to put the fix in with Dutch customs, potentially buy off a French cop and his island police force, and know exactly which hotel room to bug."

"Ah," Grimaldi said. "You're talking about none other than Willard Forsythe Everett the Third."

**7**

Bolan, Grimaldi and Tyler sat on hard wooden chairs in the dingy office that was only slightly larger than a walk-in closet. Putrid greenish paint, peeling in various spots on the walls and ceiling, gave the illusion of encroaching mold. A bulletin board with various posters and dispatches, all in French, was centered on the wall to the left of them, and a picture of the French president was framed behind Captain Le Pierre's desk. A large ceiling fan slowly oscillated above their heads, doing little to dispel the oppressive humidity and heat. Dark rings stained the armpits of Le Pierre's short-sleeved khaki shirt.

"Once again," the officer said from behind his dilapidated wooden desk, "my apologies for the incident that occurred yesterday."

"Does that mean you're going to give me back my SIG?" Grimaldi asked.

Le Pierre glared at him, then smiled and shook his head. "Unfortunately, no. I have not yet received any official word from the department of state."

"Yours or ours?" the pilot asked.

Bolan nudged Grimaldi's knee. Both he and Jack suspected that Le Pierre was being paid to look the other way and delay investigation into the ambush, so Bolan wanted to limit their encounters with the crooked gendarme. When the time was right, he'd deal with the man. Right now, they had more important matters to attend to. Still, he was cognizant of the need to put on a decent appearance of propriety in this farce of a meeting.

"I'll have to look into that," Tyler said. He'd been about as useful as the ceiling fan. "With the American State Department, that is."

"It's perfectly understandable, Captain," Bolan said. "Were you able to find out anything about the men who attacked us?"

"Island trash." Le Pierre pursed his lips, as if disgusted. "Like I told you, bandits who are under the control of a man named Arsen Boudrous. He and his bunch live in the mountains. We have had trouble with him many times, but always periodically."

"Give me back my SIG and I'll go up there and arrest him for you," Grimaldi said. "And what about that receipt for my gun that you promised me?"

Le Pierre lifted an eyebrow and frowned. "It is in the process of being prepared as we speak."

"What about the Russian guy who was with the bandits?" Bolan asked. "Any idea who he was?"

Le Pierre shook his head and frowned again. "We have not been able to determine his identity. All we know is that he appears to be European. As of late, we have been bombarded with a wave of illegal aliens."

"He must have come in the Dutch side," Grimaldi said. "So when do I get my receipt?"

Le Pierre's face twisted into a deeper frown. "I shall notify you at your hotel when it is ready."

"Captain," Bolan said, standing and offering his hand. "We came by to complete that report, as you directed us yesterday. If there's nothing further, we'll be going."

Le Pierre stared at Bolan's hand, then stood and shook it, along with Grimaldi's and Tyler's.

On the way out of the police station Grimaldi turned to look back at the sandy area leading up to the stucco walls. "What a dump. I've seen better facilities in Somalia."

"Oh, it's not so bad," Tyler said. "Plus, the captain told me they're in the process of remodeling. Mr. Everett gave them a big donation for improvements."

"I'll bet he did," Bolan said.

As THEY STOOD in front of the hotel, Tyler got a call on his cell and moved about twenty feet away. Grimaldi's eyes followed him.

"I guess boy wonder doesn't fully trust us yet," he said. "He must have a short memory, considering we saved his bacon yesterday."

"Cut him some slack," Bolan said. "He's still into doing everything by the book. You remember the book, don't you?"

"What book?" Grimaldi said, the frown changing to a grin. "Anyway," he continued. "I guess the question is really whether we trust him. Do you?"

Bolan considered for a moment, then said, "Yeah, pretty much. I think he's just a little green. I had the Farm run a routine check on him, and it came back clear. Plus, Tyler seemed pretty surprised by the ambush. I don't think he could have faked his reaction."

"Fair points." Grimaldi took a deep breath. "What's our next move?"

"Well, Hal said they were sending over some new equipment from the diplomatic post in Barbados this morning. We need to wait here for that."

Just then, Tyler terminated his call and trotted over to them. "That was Quantico. They're sending me a backup contingent of two agents because of the ambush yesterday. I'm going to the airport shortly to meet them. Want to come along?"

"No, we've got other plans," Grimaldi said. "Like trying to nail down the criminals behind all this."

Tyler's brow crinkled. "I thought we took care of them yesterday. And Captain Le Pierre said they'd pick up that Boudrous guy."

"You haven't figured things out yet, kid?" Grimaldi asked.

Tyler's jaw jutted out. "I'd appreciate it if you wouldn't call me that."

"My partner meant no disrespect," Bolan said, shooting Grimaldi a warning glance. "There may be a greater plot in the works, but we don't know much yet. Will you do one thing for us before you head to the airport?"

Tyler sighed. "What do you need?"

"Sweep your room for bugs. We found several in ours yesterday when we checked in."

"Bugs?" Tyler said.

"Yeah, and we aren't talking about the six-legged kind," Grimaldi added. "Courtesy of our buddy and island bigwig, Willard Everett III."

"But he's an American." Tyler sounded incredulous.

"Yeah, so was Al Capone," Grimaldi said.

Tyler shook his head. "Mr. Everett's been nothing but helpful to me since I arrived. Met me personally here at the hotel, and arranged for Captain Le Pierre to have one of his men escort me around the island to facilitate my search."

Grimaldi clicked his tongue. "Doesn't our little reception party yesterday tell you something? How do you think those creeps knew exactly where we were and when?"

Tyler's gaze fell to the ground as he shook his head. "I just can't believe Mr. Everett's a bad guy."

"Then you've got a lot to learn," Grimaldi said.

Bolan held his hand between them and was about to speak when his phone rang. He answered it as everyone fell silent, with Tyler and Grimaldi staring each other down. When Bolan finished talking, he put his phone back into its case and said, "Jack, we've got a message at the front desk. I think our package has arrived."

Grimaldi nodded. "About time we caught a break."

Bolan turned to Tyler. "Once you've checked out your room, why don't you take our car and pick up the other agents. We've got to look into a few things around here. We can meet later and compare notes." He held out the keys.

Tyler accepted them and muttered his thanks.

"You were pretty hard on him, Jack," Bolan said once the agent was out of earshot. "Remember, he's all the backup we have right now."

"Yeah, you're right," Grimaldi said. "We're in real trouble."

GRIMES WATCHED EVERETT brush a bit of lint off his black tuxedo, which was still on the hanger, having just been delivered to his penthouse suite. Against the far wall, the huge flat-screen television lit up with an incoming Skype call. Everett set the lint brush down and snapped his fingers for Grimes to accept the call. The boss watched intently as the image of Vince Tanner came into focus. The background was in shadows, but the man's face loomed large in front of the camera lens.

"What's the situation?" Everett asked. "Is everything secure?"

"Yes, sir. Just wanted to give you an update," Tanner said. "Everything's on schedule, as instructed."

"What about the surplus?"

"Taken care of and locked up below deck. Waiting on your orders."

Everett nodded. Grimes knew this meant that the *Xerxes*'s crew, aside from those running the ship, were secure and could be easily disposed of when the time came. A good precautionary step. Tying up loose ends early on assured a smooth operation later. The crew's fate had already been sealed when Zelenkov and his team had climbed on board.

You can't make an omelet without breaking a few eggs, Grimes thought.

"Proceed to the designated coordinates," Everett said. "Resume contact when you arrive. Go no farther until instructed. Understood?"

"Affirmative, sir," Tanner replied.

"Contact me when you get there," Everett said. He waited for Tanner's acknowledgment and then terminated the Skype call. He turned to Grimes. "How much does that damn missile weigh?"

Grimes shrugged. "Between four and five thousand pounds, plus the warhead."

"Find out exactly," Everett said. "And have the pilot factor that into the fuel consumption rate for the Osprey."

"Will do, boss," Grimes said. "But don't forget we're bringing those auxiliary fuel tanks to the *Xerxes* later tonight."

"I never forget anything. Other people do, and I have to make sure I've still got everything covered." Everett massaged his temples. His voice lowered appreciably as he added, "Understand?"

Grimes knew he'd committed a faux pas, and the boss had a low tolerance for those. Grimes swallowed and muttered an apology.

Everett waved his hand dismissively. "We can't take the

chance of the *Xerxes* not making it and ending up stranded in the Atlantic on the way to deliver the bomb." He licked his lips. "And have Rinzihov calculate the exact extent of the blast radius. Even if that V-22 is gassed up, supped up, and ready to go like a bat out of hell, I don't want to get caught in some electro-magnetic pulse on the way back to the island."

Grimes knew from his time in Iraq and Afghanistan that the Osprey was twice as fast as a helicopter. They'd be almost back to the island by the time the bomb went off. The boss didn't need to worry, but all Grimes said was, "I'll get him right on it, sir."

"How's Monk doing on the decoding?"

Grimes pursed his lips. "He says he's having some trouble."

"Bullshit!" Everett slammed his fist on the desk. "The son of a bitch is stalling. He knows what's at stake." The boss glanced at his watch with a scowl.

"Want me to lean on him a little?" Grimes asked. "I can be very persuasive."

Everett blew out a slow breath as he considered this. "No, I've got a better idea. Have someone take his daughter into one of the video rooms and slap her around a little on camera. Make him watch it."

"I can't wait to see that," Grimes said. "Want them to bang her on camera, too?"

"You're a sick fuck, you know that?" Everett shook his head. "No, nothing too severe. I don't want her messed up at this point. We may have to do this in increments. Don't want to use up our commodity too quickly. But add a little salt. Have them do a strip search. Imply that worse is coming if Daddy doesn't deliver in a hurry. We have to give ourselves room to tighten the screws if we need to."

"Understood, boss. I'll get on it right away."

Everett traced his fingers over his upper lip. "Actually, get the chopper ready to fly me inland to the compound. I'll take care of Monk's daughter myself. You can get the exact weight of that warhead while we're there."

Grimes nodded and picked up the phone.

Everett looked at his watch again. "You have those invitations delivered like I told you?"

"First thing this morning, sir," Grimes answered.

"All the new players are set up on the board," he said. "It's time for me to meet this guy Cooper face-to-face."

THE INVITATION TO ATTEND the Mr. Galaxy cocktail party was addressed to Mr. Matt Cooper and Guest. A handwritten scribble across the bottom read, *"Always good to see another American south of the equator. Come see me at the party and I'll buy you a drink—WFE III."*

Bolan looked at the desk clerk, whose obsequious smile looked about as genuine as a used car salesman's.

"Who left this for me?" Bolan asked.

"I do not know, sir," the staffer said. "It was left before I came on duty."

"And this one?" Bolan said, holding up the second note.

The clerk smiled. "That one was left by the beautiful lady in room 1204, *monsieur*. Mademoiselle Kournikova."

"The Russian babe sent us a message?" Grimaldi asked as they walked away from the hotel desk. "What's it say?"

"She wants to meet us down by the Zandi Beach Bar in twenty minutes. And watch how you speak about her. Remember, she's probably a Russian agent," Bolan said.

They walked over to the main part of the lobby, where two men in sports shirts and sunglasses were seated by the main window. One of them had a large suitcase in front of him.

"Looks like those are our boys," Bolan said.

He walked over and introduced himself. Both men stood up, introducing themselves as Miller and Wellstrom. Miller leaned close. "We have your items," he whispered.

"Fine," Bolan said. "Jack will take you up to our room, but first, I need to make a call and I need clear sky above me."

Grimaldi nodded and told the two guys to follow him. Bolan went back outside and took out his satellite phone, dialing Brognola.

"I was just getting ready to call you," the big Fed said when he picked up. "Guess what we found out?"

"It's been a long morning," Bolan said. "I'm all out of guesses."

Brognola chuckled. "Okay, here's the scoop. That picture Jack sent of the dead guy turned up a hit on Interpol. Fedor Matyelshenko, member of the Russian *Mafya*. Long prison record, mostly for violent crimes—robbery, kidnapping, extortion. Associates of late are unknown, but he was rumored to be working as a hired gun for various organized crime outfits in the motherland."

"What about the woman?" Bolan asked.

"Ah, yes, Natalia Valencia Kournikova. At least that's one of her names. She also goes by Nikita Emilienko. Definitely SVR. No intel as to why she's in the Caribbean at this time."

"It's every Russian girl's dream," Bolan said. "She wants to meet me and Jack at the bar on the beach."

"Of course." Brognola laughed.

"What can you tell me about Willard Everett III?" Bolan asked.

"Just that he's so rich he could pay off the national debt with his pocket change. He's got some kind of floating platform rig a couple miles from the shore to do the special effects for the blockbuster he's financing."

"How did he make his money?"

"The easy way. He inherited it," Brognola said. "Family's big in the oil business. Willard's old man lost a ton of money back in the '79 Iranian revolution, when the Ayatollah took over. The new leader nationalized all Willard II's oil refineries in the country. He made most of it back with other ventures, but maybe that contributed to Willard III's hard line stance on the Middle East, and Iran in particular, during his ill-fated run for the presidency. Apparently he was disappointed his presidential bid didn't gain more support among conservatives, but his stances were a little right of Attila the Hun. Now he's branching out into almost everything. Why? Is he a person of interest?"

"Yeah, something's not right with him. There are way too many people getting paid down here to keep tabs on us or look the other way without Everett being involved."

"You want us to dig a little deeper?"

"Definitely. He's up to something more than just making a movie down here. Oh, and he sent me and Jack an invitation to the Mr. Galaxy cocktail party."

"That sounds interesting." Brognola laughed again. "But you better keep Jack on a short leash in case any of those Hollywood starlets show up. Where's it at?"

"It's in the grand ballroom of the Omni tonight. Everett keeps a penthouse on top." The syncopated sound of a helicopter's blades suddenly became audible as a large craft floated overhead and landed atop the hotel. Bolan stared up at the fourteen stories, plus one, which loomed in front of him like a white concrete mountain. Four elevators, encased in vertical shafts of clear Plexiglas, ascended and descended in the center of the massive building. Bolan could almost see the ornate flourishes that decorated the penthouse on the top floor, like a gabled mansion perched on a block of white marble. "I hope to get a closer look at the suite tonight."

"Well, be careful," Brognola said. "Everett's chief of security is a guy named Edwin Grimes. He's also got another security employee named Vincent Tanner. Both are supposed to be pretty tough. They saw combat in Iraq and Afghanistan, but were discharged on generals after an incident involving the questionable killings of a bunch of noncombatants. Went to work back in Iraq as private contractors for a while with a security company called Dark Stream. Guess who owns that one."

"Our buddy Willard?"

"You got it."

"I'll keep that in mind," Bolan said. He wondered if he'd be meeting Misters Grimes and Tanner tonight, as well.

**8**

Bolan watched the parking lot through the glass elevator window as he ascended to his floor. He knew an identical set of elevators on the other side of the structure afforded a view of the beach and ocean. The ceiling of the elevator car had the fine line of a trapdoor on the upper left side. It was obviously needed for maintenance purposes, but designed for minimal obtrusiveness. An equally unobtrusive tinted bulb was set in the right rear corner. Bolan was certain it housed a PTZ camera. Everett obviously liked to keep tabs on his guests. Or perhaps the rich man had a voyeuristic streak.

The elevator stopped and the doors popped open. After routinely checking both directions in the hallway, Bolan went to his room and inserted the key.

Grimaldi was standing by the windows with Miller and Wellstrom. "I'm worried those bedbugs are back," he said, as soon as Bolan entered.

The soldier nodded. He went to the bathroom and closed the door. Once inside, he pulled out his scanning device and swept the room. It came back clear. "Hey, Jack, you got to see this," he said, opening the door.

Grimaldi nodded, and motioned for Wellstrom to stay put as he ushered Miller into the bathroom.

Bolan pointed to the suitcase the man carried. "I'm sure

whoever was watching figured out what was in there, but no sense telegraphing exactly what we have."

"Right," Grimaldi added. "Let them think it's an RPG or something."

Miller nodded in understanding and unlocked the bag, pulling open the heavy zipper. "This was the best I could do on such short notice."

He took out a .45 caliber Colt 1911 Government Model and a large, folded knife. Bolan grabbed the Espada and flipped his wrist, sending the long blade flicking outward to a locked position. Grimaldi took the Colt and examined it.

"Man, this thing's an antique." He inserted a magazine, pulled back on the slide and chambered a round. He flipped up the safety and grinned. "Just call me locked and cocked."

Bolan asked Miller what else he had.

"Some magazines filled with ammo," he said, handing over the bag.

Grimaldi rummaged through the suitcase and withdrew four magazines for his Colt and three for Bolan's Beretta. "Good thing you were able to hold on to your baby." He handed Bolan the 9 mm magazines. "I can't wait to get my SIG back."

"That'll have to wait," the soldier said, tossing him a bath towel. "Put your gun in that. Right now, we have to meet someone on the beach."

GRIMES STOOD BEHIND Herman Monk's chair. He'd already looped plastic flexicuffs around Monk's wrists, securing his arms to the chair legs. A table with a television monitor was directly in front of them. Everett stood next to the table, his hands clasped behind his back. Grimes grabbed Monk's head and adjusted his grip so he could hold the man's eyes open, forcing him to look at the screen. "Watch it," he said.

The crisp color image showed Monk's daughter, from above, slowly taking off her blouse. The girl's hair looked matted and dirty, and her bright yellow blouse was stained. She slipped it completely off and stood there in her bra. Two male guards flanked her.

"Take off your pants," one of them said. "Now."

Monk tried to look away, but Grimes exerted more pressure, forcing him to face the monitor once more.

"Please," Monk said. "Please, don't hurt her."

"We hope we won't have to," Everett said. "But that's up to you."

"Please." The man's voice was a plaintive whisper. "Please. Let her go."

The strip search continued. Grace Monk took off her slacks, now clad only in bra and panties.

One of the big guards grabbed the pants away from her and muttered, "Do the rest. Everything off."

Monk strained against Grimes's hold as the monitor showed his daughter taking off her brassiere. The girl handed the guard her bra and crossed her arms in front of her breasts.

"The rest." The guard's voice was harsh and unrelenting. "Do it."

The other guard rubbed his fingers over her bare shoulder and grinned.

"No, please," Monk said. "I'll do whatever you want. Just make them stop. Please."

Everett held the small radio to his mouth and said, "Okay, that's enough."

The guard brought his own radio up. "Roger that, sir." He turned to the girl and tossed her her clothes. "Put them back on now." The two continued to stand there watching as she got dressed. The men exchanged lascivious glances.

Everett keyed his mic again and said, "Give her some privacy."

The guards acknowledged the command and left the room. Everett slowly walked over to Monk and motioned for Grimes to release him. When Everett spoke his voice was strong, yet quiet.

"Herman, Herman, Herman," he said. "The last thing I want to do is to make you uncomfortable. I don't like to hurt people, least of all pretty young things like your daughter. But you've been shining me on."

"No." Monk shook his head. "No, I haven't, sir."

Everett sighed, then gave Monk's face a quick slap. "Don't fucking lie to me." He paused. The blow had been for effect more than to cause injury. A dismissive slap. A disciplinary measure. Grimes fingered the blackjack in his pocket and wondered if Everett would let him use it.

Fat chance, he thought. Not on the old man, but on the girl, maybe… The thought excited him. He stroked the braided leather covering the lead shot. Maybe the girl…

Everett was leaning over, his face inches from Monk's now. "Herman, don't ever lie to me again," he said in a whisper. "Do you understand?"

Monk nodded, a tear winding its way down his cheek.

"Good," Everett said, his voice still low. "I need you to break those codes on the fuses for me. Get past those safeguards. I know you can, you know you can." He patted the man's shoulder gently. "And the sooner you do this, the sooner you and Grace will be able to go home. Isn't that what you want?"

"Yes." Monk's voice sounded more like a squeak than an affirmation. More tears ran from his eyes.

Everett patted his shoulder again, then straightened up.

"Okay, get to work. I'll have one of my people bring your daughter some fresh clothes." He sniffed the air. "And some for you, as well. I'll even let you both take showers if you want. But I need those safeguards dismantled today."

"I'll do it, sir," Monk said, his face showing signs of relief. "I'll do it today."

"You'd better, Herman." Everett smiled. "Because if you don't—"

"I will, I will," Monk interrupted.

Another gentle pat, then a squeeze. Everett continued, his voice calm and reassuring, "I know you will, because if you don't, we both know what'll happen, don't we?"

BOLAN AND GRIMALDI walked from the rear of the hotel toward the pristine sand of the beach. They were both in sunglasses, swimming suits and polo shirts, with towels around their necks. Bolan carried a large beach bag that held their weapons, which were wrapped in towels folded in such a way as to allow quick trigger access.

They crossed the large patio area adjacent to the hotel and finally reached the fine white sand. A hundred yards away, the ocean waves gently lapped against the shore. The flagstone sidewalk led to a one-story, plywood building with a thatched roof. The sign advertised Zandi Beach Bar in pink-and-green letters that were outlined with neon, dormant for the moment in the bright sunshine. Grimaldi lifted his sunglasses and craned his neck.

"Relax," Bolan said. "I don't think she's there yet."

"Just checking out the scenery," Grimaldi said with a mischievous grin.

"Remember to keep your eye on the ball."

They stopped at the hut, which had an open patio with tables and a row of stools butting up to a bright red bar about thirty feet long. Bolan set the bag between their stools as they sat. An unctuous-looking guy behind the bar snaked up to them.

"What'll it be, gents?" he asked. His name tag said Jimmy.

Both men asked for a cup of coffee.

The bartender's lip lifted up on one side. "Coffee? Come on. This is paradise, gentlemen."

Bolan shrugged.

"Okeydokey," the bartender said, "but I'll have to send up to the restaurant for the java. Nobody drinks it here on the beach." He grinned again. "But I can fix you guys up with anything you want. Anything."

"That's good to know," Grimaldi said.

"Ah," a female voice said, "I see you got my note. I hope you and your friend have not been waiting for me too long."

They both looked up to see Natalia Valencia Kournikova walking toward them wearing a black-and-white bikini. Her blond hair bounced around her shoulders and her skin looked like ivory. Smooth muscle rippled as she walked, showing off a body that she obviously kept in prime shape. The huge guy with her looked equally impressive. He, too, was dressed in a skimpy black swimming suit and had superb, but bulky musculature. She held her hand toward the man accompanying her. "This is Ivan."

Bolan smiled. "Nikita, how nice to see you."

"You can say that again," Grimaldi said.

Natalia laughed. "Perhaps later. Do you swim, Mr. Cooper?"

"I do," Bolan said. "Why?"

She extended her arm and pointed to the blue ocean. "There is a raft set off the pier. Do you see it?"

He scanned the water and saw the raft bobbing up and down with the waves, a large buoy connected to each corner. He nodded.

"Let's swim out to it," Natalia said. "I have something to show you out there. Come on, let's race."

Bolan and Grimaldi exchanged glances. Grimaldi swung the beach bag with their weapons onto his shoulder and followed Bolan down to the water. Kournikova reached the sea about ten yards ahead of them, waded in thigh-deep, then dived into a cresting wave. Surfacing on the other side, she began swimming toward the raft with a strong freestyle stroke.

The moist sand sank under Bolan's bare feet as the warm water splashed over his shins. He kept going until the next wave began to crest, then he, too, dived into it. The water engulfed him and he surfaced about fifteen yards behind Kournikova. He used a butterfly stroke to close the distance, lurching through the salty water. As he drew alongside her, she increased her pace. He switched to a standard freestyle and stayed next to her. He knew he could pass her, but instead kept matching her stroke for stroke as they closed in on the raft.

"Looks like it's a tie," he said.

She smiled. "You could have beaten me. Why didn't you?"

"Maybe I'd rather we both win."

Her green eyes narrowed as she looked at him, then she surveyed the raft. It was empty. She grabbed the rope that was laced through the eyelets mounted to the side, and pulled herself up. "Come join me," she said.

Bolan swung himself up and sat beside her. He waited, but she said nothing. "I thought you had something to show me."

"I lied," she said. "But this is such a nice place. Free from any prying eyes and ears."

Bolan smiled. "There must have been bugs in your room, too."

"Bugs?" Her brow furrowed, then she laughed. "Oh, yes, listening devices. I have forgotten so much of my idiomatic American vocabulary."

"I'm getting a bit rusty on my Russian, too. Maybe we can look for areas of mutual concern and help each other."

"My thoughts exactly," she said. "Why don't you go first?"

Bolan considered his options. He knew she was SVR, and he knew the Russian *Mafya* was present on the island, as evidenced by the thug who'd tried to kill them yesterday. The question was why? And if Russian agents were here, who were they looking for? He decided to put some of his cards face-up on the table.

"One of our government analysts is missing," he said. "A man named Herman Monk. I was sent here to find him."

Kournikova tipped her head back, wringing some of the water out of her long hair. "An analyst... What does such a man do in your government?"

"He analyzes. Now it's your turn."

She waited a few more seconds, then said, "The man you killed yesterday was named Fedor Matyelshenko. He was a very bad man. What you Americans call a gangster."

Bolan nodded. "I didn't think he was a Boy Scout. But I already knew his name. Let's cut to the chase. Why are you here?"

Kournikova closed her eyes and raised her face toward the sun. "It feels so lovely, doesn't it? It's hard to believe it is so bad for your skin."

"All things are best taken in moderation," Bolan said. "An old Russian proverb. Now, how about answering my question?"

A few more moments passed, then she opened her eyes

and stared at him. "I am trying to locate a man named Andrei Rinzihov. Have you ever heard of him?"

Bolan had. Rinzihov was one of the fathers of the Soviet nuclear program. He'd been heavily involved in the Union's development of nuclear weapons, and when Communism collapsed, he'd become a free agent, peddling his assets to the highest bidder. It was rumored that he'd helped both North Korea and Iran with their nuclear ambitions. "The name does ring a bell."

"My government is very concerned that in recent years he has been selling his knowledge and talents." Her expression was totally devoid of emotion. "You no doubt heard of the plane crash a few years ago that killed many of his fellow scientists?"

"I did." A private jet transporting five top Russian physicists and experts on their nuclear program had crashed under mysterious circumstances. It was widely believed to have been an act of sabotage, perhaps perpetrated by the Russian government itself as punishment for the scientists' commercialization of their expertise.

"Well, Rinzihov disappeared shortly after that. You see, he was scheduled to be on that plane, but pulled out at the last minute. It is speculated that he was either warned of the crash or was responsible for it."

"Eliminating the competition?" Bolan said.

She laughed. "Exactly. Russia has become the land of opportunity now. Anything goes. Lately, rumors have surfaced that Rinzihov has been seen in various places on the Continent in the company of Vladimir Zelenkov." She paused. "Are you familiar with this man?"

Bolan shook his head.

"At one time he was one of our Spetsnaz." Natalia's mouth puckered in an expression of disgust. "But he left the military and began selling his talents to the *Mafya*.

We now believe that both he and Rinzihov are here and, pardon the expression, in bed together with your Mr. Everett." She smiled. "That is how you Americans like to describe things, is it not?"

Bolan grinned. He was beginning to like this woman. "Only in certain circles. We are a very tolerant society. But I've been suspicious of Mr. Everett, too. He's up to something. I just don't know what."

"So there you have it. Shall we work together to solve our problems of mutual concern?"

"Sounds like a plan. The first thing we need to do is check out some of Everett's activities around the island. Especially out there." He pointed to the horizon, where the greenish hue of the water changed to a deep blue. "You up for a little deep-sea fishing?"

"But of course," she said.

Bolan glanced at his watch. They'd been lying in the direct sunlight a little too long and he didn't want either of them to have to deal with any tropical burns. "Shall we swim back and discuss it further?"

"Yes," she said. "But let us not race this time. We should take our time. And talk."

"Sidestroke suits me fine," he said. "By the way, Everett invited me and Jack to his Mr. Galaxy party tonight. Your countryman, Mark Steel, is going to be there. Would you like to accompany us?"

She smiled as she got to her feet to dive. "Mark Steel is a pig. I knew of him when he was Allyosha Misha Snitkonoy, a member of our Olympic weightlifting team. He defected at a competition in Berlin and became the pet project of a wealthy German industrialist."

Bolan rose and stood beside her. "You didn't answer my question. Would you like to go to the party tonight as my guest?"

"Of course," she said, taking a step toward the edge of the raft. "But I should tell you that I already have my own invitation."

**9**

Bolan waded ashore and walked over to Grimaldi and Ivan, who had been watching them from the sand.

"We're going deep-sea fishing," Bolan said to Grimaldi. "And the good news is you and Kournikova get to stay in the boat while Ivan and I swim."

"Sounds like I'm getting the better of that deal," Grimaldi said. "Where you guys swimming to?"

"We're going over toward Everett's floating platform rig. Kournikova says the area's being heavily patrolled by local police boats. Something tells me that *A Slice of Heaven* might have once wandered over that way."

THE FISHING BOAT was large enough for Bolan and Ivan to change into their scuba gear in the lower cabin. When they'd shoved off thirty minutes earlier, the captain of the craft had balked at bringing them close to Everett's floating platform.

"It is forbidden," the man said. "They have police patrol boats in the area. They are armed and do not tolerate violations."

"Who's talking about tolerating?" Grimaldi said, reaching in his pocket and producing a roll of cash. "Just get us in close enough to check things out, and we'll leave if they ask us."

The captain's eyes lit up as he looked at the money, but when he reached out for it, Grimaldi pulled his hand back. "Nope, *after* we get back to the dock."

The man's venality had overridden his trepidation, and he'd agreed to take them out to the platform. He said the cops on the boats normally took a long lunch break at one o'clock.

"Good to know," Grimaldi said. "Now let's go run a blockade."

The platform initially looked like a small, dark spot on the surface of the blue water, but gradually became more defined. When they were close enough to distinguish the superstructure, Bolan and Ivan went below to get suited up. True to his word, the captain had managed to circumvent the patrols, for the moment. He stopped the boat about a hundred yards from the rig. Several men on the platform were already lining up on one of the catwalks.

"I don't know how long you guys will have," Grimaldi called into the cabin. "Looks like our friends on the platform are already on the horn." He made a show of smiling and waving at them.

Bolan motioned to Ivan, who followed him up the three steps from the cabin. Bolan did a belly roll over the far side of the boat, his splash hidden from the men on the platform rig.

"Swim quickly, boys," Kournikova shouted as he went over.

He felt the soft embrace of the warm seawater. Ivan splashed in seconds later. Bolan put a hand on his mask and blew a breath through his nose, clearing the screen. Ivan was already swimming past him, so Bolan kicked his legs, propelling himself in the direction of the rig. After they had gone about seventy-five yards, he made out the massive beams descending from the floating platform toward the darker depths below.

Ivan paused and Bolan saw him eyeing the supports, as well. The soldier pulled up beside him and pointed to his watch. Seven minutes had elapsed since they'd left the boat. Their plan was to be gone no longer than fifteen. They figured that was probably how much time they had before the absent patrol boat would be able to intercept the fishing trawler. Bolan held up his hand and signaled five minutes, and Ivan nodded.

Both men swam as quickly as they could. Bolan saw a trio of support lines descending from the center of the platform, but these weren't part of the beams. They were more like drilling cables. Or something else... He swam closer. Umbilical cords, perhaps? Did they have some submersibles or perhaps an underwater station down there?

Whatever the cables were for, their purpose was obscured by the dark waters. It was clear to Bolan that they'd have to return with better equipment. Underwater scooters, perhaps. But even with them, how far down could they safely travel? The current was beginning to pull on both of them. Going down there would be problematic in a standard hard-hat suit, let alone trying to negotiate the murkiness in scuba gear. They'd need heavy-duty diving gear—wasp suits, most likely—to explore down there.

Bolan paused and glanced upward. The underbelly of the platform looked solid and inviting. He wondered what answers it could provide.

He checked his watch again. Their five minutes were almost up.

A dark shadow flickered on the periphery of his vision. Bolan turned his head and saw a triangular wedge knifing through the water toward the platform supports. The shape twisted sideways and Bolan recognized it: a shark. Farther away three more sliced through the water.

Bolan looked upward and saw a murky cloud between him and the surface of the water. One shark swam through it, then another, and Bolan suddenly knew what it was: blood. The men on the rig above must have been pouring it over the side. A nice way to lure the school of sharks into augmenting the rig's security.

It was definitely time to leave.

He swam to Ivan and motioned toward the sharks and then in the direction of the fishing boat. Ivan's eyes widened and he began swimming as fast as he could. Bolan glanced back, hoping the freshly-poured blood would distract the animals long enough for him and Ivan to get back to the boat.

As they swam, Bolan flipped over and glanced back at the platform. He couldn't see the sharks now, but that didn't mean they were gone. All it meant was that they'd most likely left the immediate vicinity of the rig. And both men were leaving a clear trail of bubbles.

Ivan came alongside him and touched his arm, pointing upward. A large black shape moved rapidly across the surface of the water above them.

More company. A police patrol boat, no doubt. They had misjudged how much time they had. And they were still a few minutes away from their companions.

It's up to Jack to deal with those island coppers now, Bolan thought, or Ivan and I will have a real long swim back to the beach.

GRIMALDI LOWERED THE high-powered binoculars and frowned. First the helicopter, an old Russian Mi-24 Hind, had flown overhead and landed on the platform. And now these new visitors. Time was not on their side today. He turned to the fishing boat captain.

"You got a rifle on board?" he asked.

"A rifle?" The captain looked warily toward the approaching craft. "I will not permit you to shoot at the police. They have machine guns and will kill us all."

"I'm not worried about those jokers," Grimaldi said. He pointed to a large fin knifing through the water. "I'm more worried about that one."

The captain's mouth twisted downward. "A shark. This is not good."

"Tell me about it," Grimaldi said. Where there was one, there were probably more.

The police boat's siren wailed and a set of red lights blinked above the cabin. Two uniformed men with rifles stood on the bow, holding on to the metal railing as the boat flopped against the waves. When they were perhaps fifty feet away the vessel slowed, but the siren and lights stayed on. Grimaldi started to move to the prow, but Kournikova had beaten him to it. And that wasn't all. She'd taken off her bikini top. Grimaldi knew she was trying to buy Bolan and Ivan more time with a distraction, and from the look on the faces of the coppers as their boat went dead in the water twenty feet away, she was succeeding.

A loud voice came through a megaphone. "You have entered a restricted area. You must leave immediately or face arrest."

Kournikova shouted back at them in Russian, pointing with one hand while the other covered her bare breasts.

The voice on the loudspeaker stopped momentarily, then resumed, repeating the same message.

"Hey," Grimaldi called, stepping up onto the deck next to Kournikova. He figured the more eyes that were focused topside, the fewer would be scanning the water. "You guys have a lot of nerve. Can't you see my wife's lost her bikini top? We're trying to find it."

One of the island policemen came to the side of the patrol boat and stared at Kournikova.

"Watch where you're looking, buddy," Grimaldi said. "She's very modest."

The policeman's mouth dropped open, then he smiled. "Yes, I see that. Where did you lose it?"

Kournikova affected a perplexed expression and turned to Grimaldi, speaking in Russian. Although he knew very little of the language, he played along. "She says if she knew that it wouldn't be lost."

The policeman's mouth pursed. "How do you expect us to help you if you will not tell us where to look?"

"Try looking on the other side of your boat," Grimaldi said.

Several of the policemen moved to the far side of their vessel. Grimaldi heard a commotion coming from the port side of the fishing boat. He glanced behind him and saw Bolan clambering over the rail, minus his scuba gear, holding a black bikini top. He held it up and grinned. "Found it."

The men raised their weapons again and one shouted, "Who is *that?*"

"Relax," Grimaldi said. "He's my brother-in-law. On my wife's side."

Ivan climbed over next, also without his diving gear.

"And him?" the officer asked. "Who is he?"

"He's my brother," Grimaldi said. He took in the policeman's skeptical expression and added, "We're twins. He got all the muscles and I got all the brains."

The policeman shook his head in exasperation. "No matter. You must leave now. Immediately."

"Okay, okay," Grimaldi said, turning to the fishing boat captain. "Let's get the hell out of here."

The man fired up the engine and began backing away from the patrol boat.

Bolan walked up the stairs to the foredeck and handed Kournikova her top.

"Here you go, *sis*," he said with a wide grin.

GRIMES WATCHED AS Everett lowered his high-powered binoculars and turned to face him. They stood on the catwalk, a mild sea breeze blowing over them. Everett didn't look pleased. "The Russians have teamed up with the Americans. Who ordered that blood to be dropped?"

"Unknown," Grimes said, glad it hadn't been him. "I can check."

"Do that. And tell the dumb son of a bitch not to do it again. Not unless I personally authorize it."

"Understood, boss," Grimes said. "I can have the police stop the fishing boat and bring them back here if you want."

Everett's frown deepened. "Negative. The *last* thing I want is another incident like we had with that goddamn yacht."

Grimes turned to leave. The last thing *he* wanted was to be the focus of another one of his boss's rants.

"Hold on," Everett said. "I wonder how much they saw, and where they saw it from." He walked over to the control panel and gazed at the array of monitors. "Play back the video streams for cameras seven and eight for the last twenty minutes."

The technician at the controls nodded. He pressed a few buttons and brought up the feeds. The picture showed stagnant, murky water. Everett asked the technician to fast-forward, then stop as two men in scuba gear appeared, swimming near the support beam. He tapped the screen.

"Cooper and the Russian. Snooping around." He rubbed his cheeks. "How many more of the warheads are down there?"

"Only one," Grimes said. "But the going's slower now. Taking more time."

"Time is something I don't have a lot of," Everett said. "Damn it. I wonder what those bastards saw? I didn't see any gamma ray detectors."

"You want me to increase the number of patrol boats?"

Everett continued to stroke his face, then shook his head. "No, those cretins are basically useless, anyway. Make sure that next recovery is well-disguised before it's brought to the compound."

Grimes nodded. "What do you want to do about Cooper and the others?"

The boss locked eyes with him. "You ever see Jerry Quarry box?"

"No, sir." Here we go again, he thought. Another boxing metaphor.

"Yeah, I forgot. Before your time," Everett said. "Quarry was a great counterpuncher. Here, I'll show you. Put up your guard."

Grimes warily assumed a boxing stance. Everett frowned and moved Grimes's hand to a set position. "His greatest strength was in waiting for his opponent to make the first move." The boss grabbed Grimes's left arm and stretched it out, ducking under it. "Then he'd step inside and belt the guy with short, powerful hooks." Still holding Grimes's arm, Everett pivoted and sent a quick, hard left into his abdomen.

Grimes felt the power of the blow and sank to one knee. His gut hurt like hell, but he knew Everett had most likely pulled the punch. The rich little prick was short, but he could hit.

"But he couldn't win the big ones. If he hadn't lost sight of his major strength during those fights, he would've been heavyweight champ." Everett helped Grimes over to a chair. "Quarry died probably thinking about what might have been."

Yeah, right, Grimes thought. How did I end up working for this nut job, anyway?

"But back to the case in point," Everett continued. "Remember what I said about keeping your friends close and your enemies closer?"

Grimes managed a nod.

"Let's give Mr. Cooper enough rope to hang himself," the boss said. "Have some extra men in the hotel during the big party. And start some underwater patrols around the platform, especially at night."

"Will do." Grimes was finally starting to get his breath back.

Everett smiled down at him.

"You think..." Grimes paused and took another shallow breath "...he'll try something at the party?"

Everett's smile widened. "I'll be disappointed if he doesn't."

## 10

As they walked back to the hotel from the docks, Bolan and Kournikova separated themselves from the others and took out their respective satellite phones.

She's probably giving a sitrep to her superiors in Moscow, Bolan thought as he dialed Brognola's number. The big Fed answered with a brisk "About time you called."

"If I didn't know better, I'd say it sounds like you miss me," Bolan drawled.

"Yeah, right," Brognola said with a laugh.

"Any new developments?" Bolan asked.

"We know that the Feds sent a contingent of more agents down that way. I figured that was good news. Give you guys some extra help."

Between meeting up with Kournikova and undertaking the scuba diving mission, Bolan hadn't had a chance to touch base with Tyler. Now he was curious to know how the pickup had gone, and to check on the FBI man's latest activities. "It could be. That Tyler guy's a little inexperienced, and you know how much patience Jack has for greenhorns."

"Yeah, I can imagine. You find out anything concrete yet?"

"We did a little underwater exploration around Willard Everett's platform and caused some waves."

"That floating rig he's got down there? Give me the coordinates and I'll set up some round-the-clock satellite surveillance."

"That'd be good. Something's up with him, I just don't know what. We'll probably go back again tonight for a closer look. Might need some shark repellant, though."

"Sharks? Are you sure Everett is responsible for them?"

"His men are keeping them interested by dumping blood in the water. And besides the big fish, there's way too much security around that rig for some kind of movie set. I texted you two names earlier. You get them?"

"I did," Brognola said. Bolan heard the shuffling of papers over the phone. "Okay, here. Vladimir Zelenkov, ex-Spetsnaz, was accused of too much brutality during their Chechnya campaign, if you can believe that, and *retired* from the military. He was also involved in that botched hostage rescue at the opera house. Got recruited by the Russian mob soon after and has a reputation for getting the job done."

"So I've heard," Bolan said. "What about Andrei Rinzihov? Find out anything I don't already know?"

Brognola sighed heavily. "No, I think you've got as much info on him as we do. Jesus, if he's involved there must be some kind of connection to nukes. You finding anything along those lines?"

"Kournikova says he's affiliated with Zelenkov now."

"Probably as a measure of self-preservation. Of the six Soviet nuclear pioneers who were selling out to the highest bidders, he's the only one left. The others mysteriously perished in a plane crash in the motherland."

"I remember that one," Bolan said. "And Rinzihov was supposed to be on the same flight. Anyway, Natalia says she's down here to look into him."

"Natalia? Sounds like you two might be getting pretty

close," Brognola said. "But it makes sense they'd send somebody down there to try and finish the job. Still, remember that she's SVR. I'd trust her about as far as I could throw her."

Bolan caught a glimpse of the exceptionally beautiful woman perhaps forty feet away. She was talking animatedly on her phone. Their eyes met for a moment and she smiled and waved.

"Don't forget," Brognola said, "she's probably racked up more kills than the Red Baron ever did."

"I'll bet she has," Bolan said, as he waved back to her.

WILLARD FORSYTHE EVERETT III deftly tied the knot in his black bow tie. Grimes was standing by, but he knew the boss preferred to tie them himself. Grimes, on the other hand, could never get the hang of it and resorted to clip-ons in the rare instances when he had to dress formally. His tuxedo jacket was specially made to allow for proper concealment of the shoulder rig that held the Smith & Wesson Bodyguard .380 that he liked to carry for such occasions. Small and light enough not to be noticed, except by the trained eye, and still packing a good wallop with six in the mag and one in the pipe. He wondered if he'd get a chance to use it tonight on Cooper.

"Everything set with the extra guards by the penthouse and in the stairwells?" Everett asked.

"Two of Zelenkov's boys are stationed in each stairwell with a couple of Boudrous's thugs, and a three-man patrol of ours is roving the fifteenth floor. They have an access card to get in the penthouse if necessary, but they have been briefed not to enter unless it's an emergency, and even then, not without authorization."

Everett pulled the looped portion of the tie through the knot and tugged it to a perfect bow. "Sounds like you've got it all covered," he said. "Let's go down and join the festivities and see what the evening brings."

Grimes smiled and licked his lips. He hoped that Cooper would try something, and he also hoped he'd get a chance to go head-to-head with the son of a bitch. It would be a good release for all the tension he'd built up from taking Everett's shit. "Yeah," he said. "Let's hope."

BOLAN AND GRIMALDI, clad in black and white tuxedos, respectively, stood by the elevators and watched as Kournikova and Ivan made their way toward them through the moderately crowded lobby.

"You look lovely," Bolan said, taking in Kournikova's low-cut blue evening gown. Ivan stood next to her, looking like a gorilla with a shaved head in a tux.

"You look very handsome as well, Cooper," Natalia said with a smile.

"Thanks." Bolan offered her his arm. "Shall we?"

"Most assuredly." She hooked her hand around his elbow.

Ivan and Grimaldi exchanged glances and fell in behind them.

The Mr. Galaxy party was in the Omni's main ballroom, which was resplendent with beige walls periodically bisected by fine white pillars. In front of each pillar was a large vase containing luscious green leaves caressing a floral spray. Silver netting was artfully draped around several chandeliers suspended from the ceiling. In stark contrast to the palatial effect, several large flat-screen televisions had been positioned around the room, playing a continuously looping video about the Mr. Galaxy contestants, past and present, and centering on former bodybuilding champion Mark Steel. The film periodically advised that Steel had recently traded bodybuilding for a movie career. He was currently set to make his debut in *Undersea Warriors*, a motion picture from Everett Unlimited, the new production company of W. F. Everett III. "It's guaranteed to be a blockbuster," the announcer kept repeating.

"Looks like quite a shindig," Grimaldi said.

"And there's the undersea warrior himself," Bolan said, pointing to the massively proportioned Mark Steel, who was standing in the center of the room with a cocktail glass in one hand and a beautiful starlet in the other.

Grimaldi moved closer to Bolan. "I don't see Tyler," he whispered.

"He texted me," the soldier said. "He and his two new backup agents are lying low until I need their assistance for my little visit upstairs."

Grimaldi nodded. "Smart move."

"Mr. Cooper, I presume," a voice behind them said. "I've been hearing a lot about you."

Bolan turned to face a short, but powerfully built man with a wide grin and his right hand extended. A taller guy with dark hair and equally broad shoulders stood next to him. Bolan recognized them both from the pictures Brognola had emailed.

"I'm Will Everett," the man said.

Bolan shook Everett's hand. He could tell the other man was exerting a bit of an extra squeeze, so the soldier returned the effort. They stood locked there for a few seconds, each sizing the other up, until Everett released his grip and cocked a thumb back toward his companion. "This is my chief of security, Edwin Grimes."

Grimes's handshake was smooth, but with a hint of power.

"Please introduce me to your friends," Everett said.

Bolan made the introductions and Everett made a show

of bringing Kournikova's hand to his lips for a quick kiss. "It's always a pleasure to meet such a beautiful woman."

She smiled graciously and immediately abandoned Bolan's side for Everett's.

The soldier watched, pleased that the evening was all going according to plan.

For the moment, that is, he added mentally.

"So tell me," Everett said to him. "Are you enjoying your stay here on St. Francis?"

"What's not to enjoy?" Bolan replied. "It's a beautiful place."

"Beats the hell out of the weather in Chicago," Everett said. "Or are you based out of someplace nice, like Washington?" he added with a wink.

"I travel a lot," Bolan said.

Everett nodded. Before he could say anything else, Kournikova asked to be introduced to Mark Steel.

Everett paused and took a breath. "Certainly."

"Get ready," Bolan said as he watched Kournikova conversing with the bodybuilder in their native language.

The planned diversion should be easier to set up than anticipated, he thought as he signaled to Grimaldi and Ivan that he was ready to head for the exit. A loud laugh, followed by more Russian, emanated from Steel, with Kournikova's soft laughter as an accompaniment. The starlet on Steel's arm was laughing, as well.

One big happy party, Bolan thought. Until now.

Grimaldi moved forward, assuming a cocky strut, with Ivan trailing behind him.

"You know, you're big, but you don't look so bad," Grimaldi told Steel. "I heard those bodybuilder muscles are all for show. Is that right?"

Steel stopped laughing and turned toward him. "What

are you saying?" The Russian had obviously had a bit too much to drink already.

"I'm saying," Grimaldi continued in a loud voice, "that I know somebody who could beat you at arm wrestling. Unless you're afraid we'll find out that those big biceps are only for show."

"I'll show you *for show*," Steel said, pushing the starlet away and stepping toward him. "I'll break your arm like a twig."

"Break *my* arm?" Grimaldi flashed a grin. "I don't think so. Anyway, I wasn't talking about me. I meant my brother here." He pointed at Ivan, who had stepped up beside him.

"Your brother?" Steel's face registered surprise and wariness as he sized up Ivan.

"Yeah," Grimaldi said. "We're twins. I got all the brains and he got all the muscles."

Steel stared at Ivan, who was a bit taller than the muscleman, but not quite as wide.

"Go ahead," Everett said. "Let's see who's really the bigger man." He turned to Grimes. "Clear off one of those tables."

It was working better than Bolan had hoped. Ivan knew what he was supposed to do—posture and show a lot of reticence before finally sitting down opposite Steel. Then it would be up to him to keep the arm-wrestling contest going for as long as he could. Hopefully, the whole thing would draw everyone's attention for the next fifteen minutes or so.

Bolan slipped out of the ballroom and texted Tyler that he was on the move. He had the phone set to vibrate, and felt the buzz of Tyler's reply a few seconds later. When Bolan got to the elevators, the FBI man was already there. The two didn't acknowledge one another as the elevator doors opened and they both got on. They rode up to the third floor and Bolan stepped off as Tyler pressed the lobby button. As the doors closed, Bolan removed a thin, six-inch piece of flat metal from his pocket and glanced down each hallway.

No one around. Good.

He turned back toward the elevator. He could hear the car descending. He started his count as he turned and pressed the metal blade into the round hole in upper part of the door—the release pin. The elevator door popped open, revealing the thick Plexiglass wall enclosing the shaft. Bolan glanced down in time to see the car ascending from the lobby.

The view through the glass had already acquainted Bolan with the design of the top of the elevator car. It was quite standard, equipped with the lifting mechanism. Two sets of parallel cables were lopped through the pulley system to raise and lower the elevator. When the car was five feet below him, rising rapidly, he swung inside the shaft and jumped between the cables, landing on the roof of the car. The momentum caused him to stumble slightly before he regained his balance, but he avoided striking the wall. The car came to a stop on the third floor, and he heard the doors open, then close. He stamped his foot on the roof twice, indicating to Tyler to press the button for the fourteenth floor. The penthouse, he knew, was on the fifteenth floor, which was inaccessible from below without a special key. Tyler's response, three knocks, signaled that he'd pressed the button.

At least the kid hadn't said anything about the little break and enter caper that Bolan had planned. Maybe he was wising up faster than Grimaldi had predicted.

STEEL HAD REMOVED his tuxedo jacket and was flexing his pectoral muscles, making the ruffles on the front of his white shirt dance. He glared at Ivan, who met his gaze calmly. Wanting to buy Bolan as much time as possible, Grimaldi stepped beside Ivan and pointed to Steel's fluttering chest muscles.

"You ever thought about doing commercials?" he said. "If this movie flops, you've got a great future with Victoria's Secret."

"What?" Steel asked, his mouth twisting downward.

"Bra commercials." Grimaldi cupped his hands in front of his chest. "What size do you run? About a 55 B?"

Kournikova giggled.

Steel, obviously enraged, reached for Grimaldi's hands, but Ivan grabbed Steel's left wrist.

"First, you deal with me," he said.

Steel pulled his arm away and the two men went back to their glaring contest.

A good, old-fashioned stare-down, Grimaldi thought. This is working out better than we'd hoped. Pretending to adjust his jacket, he glanced surreptitiously at his watch. Plenty of time. The two men hadn't even sat down yet.

WHEN THE ELEVATOR stopped at the fourteenth floor, Bolan noted that the shaft extended a good forty feet above him, but he couldn't see an opening to the penthouse. A series of metal bars forming an X separated this elevator shaft from the one next to it. He took out his small flashlight and shone it upward. As he traced the wall of the adjacent shaft, the beam swept over a closed elevator door about six feet up and to his left. Clearly, only one elevator shaft opened onto the fifteenth floor. And it wasn't the one Bolan had chosen.

Still, the single-elevator access made sense. Everett probably had a key-controlled override installed in that car so he could summon the elevator and keep it solely for his own use.

Bolan moved across the top of the car and grabbed the X beams just as the elevator began its quick descent. He watched it going down toward the lobby, then carefully adjusted his feet and gripped the angular beams, climbing toward the closed door. Within seconds, he had established a precarious position on the metal braces. Reaching across the empty space with his left arm, he was able to grab hold of the metal frame that housed the elevator doors where they would retract into the wall. He placed the toe of his left dress shoe onto the thin, concrete ledge along the bottom of the door frame. It was perhaps an inch wide.

With one leg still braced on the support beam, Bolan was too spread out to reach the metal rod that opened and closed the doors. Adjusting his stance, he managed to wiggle a few inches closer, and tried again for the rod. His fingertips brushed against it, but he was still too far away. The effort made his foot slip off the small ledge, but his strong grip on the X beam kept him from falling. It was a long way down, he noticed, as his left foot and hand swung out over the dark shaft. He took a deep breath and tried again for purchase on the tiny ledge. He managed to reestablish his foothold, but the distance was still too great to allow him to get a safe grip on the elevator doors.

The clock's ticking, he thought. Bolan gathered his strength for an all-or-nothing lunge. He hung suspended in space for a split second before his fingers closed around the metal rod. Pulling himself forward, he got both his feet onto the ledge and flattened himself against the door.

Now would be a good time to get this thing open, he thought. Moving in small increments, Bolan extracted the thin metal pick from his pocket once again, but as he brought it up to insert it in the door release mechanism, it slipped from his fingers, cascading downward for six or seven seconds before clattering on top of the elevator car at lobby level. He stayed frozen, hoping the noise hadn't alerted anyone.

After about thirty seconds, he cautiously reached upward with his right hand, nimbly exploring the metal catch that locked the door rods in place. Ten more seconds ticked away on his mental clock before he managed to find and press the right mechanism. The tension in the rod slackened and he felt the twin doors pop apart ever so slightly. He worked his fingers into the expanding crack between the doors and pushed, shifting his weight forward and landing on his hands and knees on the plush carpeting of the penthouse floor. He was in a small foyer with doors on either side. Straight ahead of him, a hallway led to another door. Although the foyer was lit, the hallway was dark. Bolan glanced to his left and saw there was no button to summon the elevator. Instead, the ornate housing plate displayed only a slot for a key.

Guess I'll be taking the stairs, he thought as he let the elevator slide closed behind him. He moved down the hallway. The door at the end was locked, but it succumbed to the tip of Bolan's knife in half a minute. He cautiously stepped into the room and discovered a massive, darkened den replete with sofas, leather chairs, an enormous flatscreen television, and a huge, cluttered desk off to the left side. Bolan paused in the doorway, letting his eyes adjust to the darkness. He wished he had a pair of night vision goggles, but obtaining proper equipment had been somewhat problematic on this trip. He slipped his small, but powerful LED flashlight out of his pocket and swept the room.

Nothing moved. He scanned the ceiling for cameras and saw two small, opaque PTZ bubbles. If the cameras were being monitored and the lenses were equipped with infrared filters, Everett and his staff would soon know he was in the penthouse, if they didn't know already.

STEEL AND THE OTHER big Russian man faced each other across the cleared-off table, fists locked. They'd been arm wrestling for a good five minutes, Grimes noted, and so far neither had budged. Steel's face was covered with sweat and the veins along his temples and neck stuck out. The other man was obviously feeling the strain, too. They had both removed their tux jackets before starting, and now their white shirts looked ready to split apart at any second.

Everett seemed to be eating this stuff up. He stood close to the pair, like some impromptu coach, egging his boy on, making a big show of it. Grimes knew the boss was aware that Cooper was probably trying to sneak upstairs during this charade.

Grimes felt the vibration of his cell phone on his hip. He reached down and removed it from its holder.

Intruder is in penthouse, the text read.

So Cooper had gained access that quickly. The guy was good. Of course, the way he'd handled Boudrous's goons and Matyelshenko at the plateau ambush had been an indication that this was no neophyte. But now the real trap was about to be sprung.

Let's see how he does upstairs on his own and unarmed, Grimes thought. Unless he'd managed to sneak a gun under that tight-fitting tuxedo.

Proceed with interception, he texted back. Capture alive if possible.

Roger that.

Grimes caught Everett's eye as he looked up, and gave his boss a slight nod. Everett returned it and his smile grew wider.

"Come on, come on," he yelled. "You two guys gonna

sit there and play all night? I'll make it interesting. Fifty grand to the winner."

That's the boss for you, thought Grimes. Always raising the stakes.

BOLAN HAD JUST gotten to the desk when he heard the elevator doors sliding open almost noiselessly behind him. He moved swiftly to the den door and flattened himself against the wall next to it.

A gloved hand holding a Taser extended through the doorway. Bolan saw the profile of a man wearing night vision goggles. The soldier quickly depressed his flashlight switch with his thumb and shone it directly into the man's face, causing him to recoil. The front of the Taser exploded, sending the two wired prongs flying uselessly into space.

Bolan grabbed the man's arm, pulling him forward and simultaneously sending a hard kick into the guy's solar plexus. When he grunted and slumped forward, Bolan snatched the Taser from his grasp, then shone his flashlight into the narrow hallway. Two more men in night vision goggles were running in his direction. Bolan swung the bright beam into the eyes of the next man in the line just as the guy yelled, "Freeze. Put up your hands!" This one held a Glock 21.

If you're going to shoot, shoot, Bolan thought. Don't talk about it.

He stepped forward, stripping the expended cartridge from the front of the Taser, which he used to stun the second man. Bolan caught a glimpse of the third assailant pulling off his goggles as he removed his own Glock from its holster, so the soldier pushed the second man into him, which blocked the shot that echoed in the narrow hallway. Bolan's fist collided with the third man's temple. He stumbled into the wall and staggered forward, still holding the Glock. Bolan dropped the Taser and delivered an uppercut to his chin, and the third man collapsed in a heap.

Bolan kicked the Glock away from him and grabbed the second man's gun. Satisfied that these three were down for the count, he turned and lifted the first fallen adversary out of the doorway, stopping to pluck the night vision goggles from his face, and slammed the door shut as he stepped back into the den. As Bolan ran back to the desk he saw what had piqued his interest before: a camera fitted with a long lens.

Better not to leave totally empty-handed, he thought as he snatched it from the desktop. He slipped the camera strap over his head so it was secured under his right arm as he ran. More movement came from behind him, and an unknown voice yelled, "Halt!"

Another guy who'd rather talk than shoot, Bolan thought as he fired a quick round from the Glock through the doorway. He sprinted across the room toward an adjacent hallway that appeared to lead toward the corner of the building. As with the rest of the hotel, there were likely emergency stairwells on both sides.

At least I hope there are, he thought, as several rounds zipped past, puckering the wall next to him. He crouched and kept moving, suddenly aware that he'd trapped himself in an elongated kill zone. He noticed a gymnasium on his right, sealed off by two metal doors with large glass windows.

No wonder Everett was in such great shape. He didn't even have to drive to the gym.

Bolan spied an open door to his left. He curled inside it and switched the Glock to his left hand and extended the gun around the jamb, exposing as little of his body as possible.

The three men had recovered and were rushing down the hall toward him.

Now they're the ones in the kill zone, Bolan thought as he squeezed off two rounds at the center mass of the first man. The guy took two more steps and stumbled.

Bolan elevated his aim, acquiring a sight picture of the second man. He squeezed off another round and saw the man's goggles explode as his head jerked backward. He collapsed on top of the first man, who was trying to get up.

Body armor, thought Bolan. He fired two more rounds at the third guy, who ducked through the gym doors and fired back half a magazine.

Bolan crouched and shot the first man in the forehead as he aimed his pistol in the soldier's direction.

More rounds tore into the wall near Bolan's head.

Too close for comfort.

He returned fire, estimating that the Glock had a 13 round capacity. He'd lost track of how many of them were gone. Seven, maybe? No time to drop the mag and check. He knew his assailant might decide to take the initiative and charge forward. Or the guy could stay put and wait for the backup that was most likely on its way.

Bolan fired one round down the hallway. The man returned fire.

Four shots. This guy wasn't worried about running low on ammo. Bolan timed the sequence of the shots as he got ready to spring forward. He figured he had five rounds left, so he fired off two behind him as he dashed down the hall toward the final doorway. Hopefully, it would lead to that emergency exit he was counting on.

Bolan veered slightly to his right. In a highly stressful firefight, the shooter's rounds tended to go down and to the left. Of course, that was based on the assumption that the guy was right-handed. It would be just my luck to draw a southpaw, Bolan thought as several more rounds zipped by him. He dived the last three feet into the adjoining room, doing a somersault and then rolling to his right again.

Bolan lay prone, stretching the Glock out in front of him. He reached up and flipped down the visor for the night vision goggles, and the darkened hallway suddenly became crystal clear in varying hues of green. Two men were running toward him. Bolan squeezed off one round, catching the first guy in the left thigh. A dark spray burst from the man's pant leg. Bolan adjusted his sight picture and shot the second man high in the chest, hoping the round would penetrate even if this guy was wearing a vest. The man jerked back as if he'd been hit, then kept on coming, firing rounds from his handgun as he ran.

Bolan elevated his sight picture, zeroing in for a head shot, and squeezed off another round. This time the green-hued picture showed an explosion of dark mist around the man's head. Momentum carried him one more step before he crumpled.

The slide was locked back on Bolan's Glock. Empty and no new magazine. He debated rushing down the hall to retrieve one from one of his fallen adversaries, but the thought of wasting time searching made the move seem unwise. Seconds later, this decision was vindicated as a new set of rounds whizzed by him. Bolan managed to swing the heavy wood door closed, and twist the lock.

Good thing Willard likes his privacy, he thought.

He found himself in a modestly furnished bedroom: dresser, chair, bed. Bolan ran across the room and began searching for an emergency exit, but all he found was a full-length mirror and a solid wall.

He heard yelling and footfalls in the hallway, then someone tried the doorknob. A body crashed against it seconds later, but the lock held…for the moment, anyway. Bolan glanced down at the Glock in his hand and then to the wall in front of him.

No ammo, no exit.

GRIMALDI FELT SWEAT cascading down his body inside his shirt. The two big guys had been at it for a good ten minutes, but neither seemed to be getting the upper hand. He hoped Bolan had found something worthwhile on his little expedition. Jack hoped even more that his colleague was on his way back by now.

He moved next to Kournikova. "How much longer do you think Ivan can hold out?" he whispered.

"As long as he needs to," she said. "Steel is an oaf. Ivan is playing with him. I told him to draw it out."

Grimaldi checked out the two contestants for himself. If Ivan was playacting he should get an Academy Award nomination for sure. The veins in both their faces, necks and arms looked as if they'd been filled with collagen.

Grimaldi locked eyes with Everett, who seemed to have noticed his conversation with the Russian agent. The rich man grinned and yelled, "Come on, somebody do something! I'll make it a hundred grand."

A hundred thousand, thought Grimaldi. Damn. He was tempted to jump in and offer to arm wrestle the winner.

With Everett's pronouncement, Mark Steel leaned forward, obviously trying to exert the pressure needed to beat his opponent. Ivan shifted his weight, too, their heads almost touching as they continued to snort in each other's face.

I hope they didn't forget their breath mints, Grimaldi thought, trying to ease his worry with a bit of humor. Still, he knew Bolan could take care of himself in virtually any situation and come out on top.

Besides, he thought. This is just a simple recon break-in. Pretty much routine. What could go wrong?

BOLAN MOVED OVER to the large window and tore away the curtains. In the distance, the twinkling lights of the harbor greeted him. No inviting ledge outside. He looked to the side, craning his neck to see that the roof was about fifteen feet above him. Even if he could break the glass, he had no way to secure a rope to the side of the building. Climbing up—or down—wasn't an option.

The door shook in its frame. His assailants would be gaining access in seconds. He shoved the dresser onto its side, sliding it over to brace the beleaguered door. That might buy him a few more precious seconds.

Bolan scanned the walls again. He had to be missing something. Everett wouldn't have a penthouse with no emergency exits. If the elevator went out of service, there had to be another way down, aside from rappelling or paragliding. Bolan's eyes landed on the mirror again. He ran to it and tapped his knuckle against the surface. It produced a hollow sound, suggesting there was no wall behind it. This wasn't a mirror at all, but a window. This must be the guest bedroom, Bolan realized as he smashed the Glock against the glass. So much for Everett's voyeurism.

The pane shattered, revealing a small room containing a couple folding chairs. More importantly, Bolan spotted a door at the far end. He stepped through the frame and reached the door in three quick steps, grabbing one of the chairs on the way. A solid strip of light shone through the gap at the bottom of the door, showing no signs of movement on the opposite side.

Still no guarantees there won't be another reception party, Bolan thought as he twisted the knob. But staying in the penthouse meant certain capture or death.

He dropped the magazine in the Glock just enough to release the slide forward. The gun was empty, but anyone he might meet didn't have to know that. He took off the night vision goggles and slipped them into his inner jacket pocket. Keeping the Glock in his right hand and grabbing the chair with his left, Bolan pushed the door open and found himself in a corridor leading to a stairwell. He paused, listening, but didn't take the time to push the door flat against the wall.

He realized his mistake seconds later as he heard a crack and felt the prongs of a Taser hitting his body. He immediately began to seize up, but the momentum of his initial movement, coupled with the spinning motion he'd executed as he'd stepped through the door, allowed him to thrust the chair behind him as he fell. It struck the extended wires and dislodged one of the hooked prongs from Bolan's jacket, stopping the flow of electrical current.

Bolan felt the immobilizing tension in his muscles slacken and cease as he hit the floor. His assailant stood over him, still holding the Taser.

In the instant it took the man to realize the circuit had been broken, Bolan had already thrust his left foot into his groin. The man tipped forward onto Bolan. The guy was large and strong, and he also had a dominant position. The soldier, however, had the initiative, and while his attacker was momentarily disabled, Bolan smashed the Glock into the side of the man's head twice, then tossed the pistol away. He grabbed him under the arms, shifting his foe's weight off himself and simultaneously twisting out from under him. As the man tried to get to his knees, Bolan's fist connected with his jaw.

Jumping to his feet, the soldier delivered a solid kick to the man's liver. His opponent grunted in pain and flattened out, temporarily incapacitated.

At the periphery of his vision Bolan saw two more men running up the stairs. Both held Glock semiautomatic pistols. Bolan grabbed the man spread out before him and hurled him over the railing, sending him down onto the other two. The flying man hit the first guy, causing his Glock to discharge. Both of them fell backward in a heap toward the third man, who had been trying to aim his gun at Bolan. The collision caused him to depress the trigger of his weapon also, but so far both errant shots had missed their intended target.

Bolan vaulted over the handrail and landed on the stairs. He leaped toward the tangle of bodies and snared the second man's Glock, twisting it free. He lashed back with the pistol, striking the guy's temple, so hard that his eyes rolled back in his head.

The third man tried to bring his Glock in front of Bolan's face, but the Executioner parried it with his left hand and shot the man under the chin.

A bloody mist sprayed outward.

Despite the ringing in his ears from all the gunfire, Bolan registered a cacophony above and behind him. The men in the penthouse had broken through. He scrambled down the remaining stairs toward the next level. Another figure appeared around a corner and Bolan put two rounds into his chest and neck. As the guy fell forward, the soldier put a third round into his head.

He took the stairs two and three at a time, glancing behind him every few seconds.

Bullets whizzed past him. As Bolan rounded another corner he fired a shot upward, hoping it would hold them off. He managed to get his cell phone out and pressed the preset number for Tyler.

The FBI man answered on the first ring. "What do you need?"

"A little help would be nice," Bolan said, stopping at the door to the eleventh floor. Lucky eleven. He caught a bit of movement above him and fired another round.

"They shooting at you?" Tyler asked.

"Yeah."

"What can I do?"

Bolan's impaired hearing made Tyler's voice sound a million miles away. "Bring the elevator up to eleven," he shouted. "Now." He saw another trace of movement on the stairway and fired again.

Tyler mumbled something that Bolan couldn't discern. He put the phone back in his pocket and slipped through the door. He saw the elevators in the middle of the hallway. A fifty-yard dash. He had no doubt his pursuers would be trying to gauge his movements. He pushed open the door he'd just come through a crack, and fired three more rounds into the stairwell. All for show, he knew.

This weapon was a Glock 21, as well. Twelve-round magazine and one in the pipe made thirteen. He'd done better at keeping track of the expended rounds this time, and estimated that he had two left. If Tyler was on the way up from the lobby, and he didn't encounter any interruptions, Bolan guessed that the FBI man would reach his floor in about thirty seconds.

Time enough for a non-Olympic speed sprint, he thought. But then again, in the Olympics they didn't have to worry about outrunning a bullet.

He fired one more round to give himself the extra edge and ran down the hallway toward the elevators.

One round left. Twenty yards to go…fifteen… Turning, Bolan saw the stairwell door being pulled open.

Ten yards left.

He twisted as he ran, firing his last round in the direction of the door.

It slammed shut.

Five yards…

Bolan was at the elevators now and saw the middle set of doors opening. He dived inside and saw Tyler stretch his hand out and fire off a quick, 3-round burst with Bolan's Beretta 93R. The FBI agent pulled his arm back as the door closed and the car descended.

Tyler's grin was a mile wide. "I really like this gun," he said, holding up the Beretta.

"Just don't forget where you got it," Bolan said, straightening his jacket. He unslung the camera he'd taken from Everett's penthouse and handed it to the agent. "Secure this and tag up with me at the safe house, as planned. And here are a couple more souvenirs." He handed over the now-empty Glock and the night vision goggles.

Tyler's eyes looked ready to pop out of their sockets, but he shoved everything into his briefcase, closed it and nodded.

Bolan watched as the numbers descended along the lit display above. In ten more seconds, the car slowed to a stop and the doors slid open. Lobby level never looked so good, he thought as he adjusted his tie and walked calmly back to the ballroom.

## 11

Bolan waded through the crowd to Grimaldi's side. The arm-wrestling contest was in its final stages. Both Ivan and Steel were covered with sweat, their shirts pulled taut over their hulking bodies.

"Who's winning?" Bolan asked.

Grimaldi gave him a once-over and smiled. "Looks like we did."

Bolan caught Ivan's eye and the big Russian winked. He emitted a keening, primordial growl and Steel's arm began to sink lower and lower toward the tabletop. Just as the back of his hand was slammed down, Steel stood up and jerked away.

He muttered something in Russian.

"What did he say?" Grimaldi asked Kournikova.

"The pig says Ivan cheated."

Grimaldi stepped forward, waving his arms. "You lost, Steel, fair and square."

"Get away from me!" Steel's mouth drew down into a fierce scowl. "Before I break you in half."

"Hey, buddy," Grimaldi said, so close now their chests almost bumped. "Nobody likes a sore loser."

"I'll show you a poor loser," Steel said, reaching for a champagne bottle on an adjacent table. He grabbed Grimaldi's lapel with one hand and the neck of the bottle with the other. As he swung the bottle back, Bolan stepped forward, blocked Steel's right arm and delivered a picture-perfect right cross to the Russian bodybuilder's jaw.

Steel's eyes rolled upward and his upper body gave a jerking twitch. A second later the bottle slipped from his slack fingers, and his knees folded as he fell onto the tiled floor.

Grimaldi brushed off his jacket and grinned widely. "I guess that settles that."

Everett strolled over and looked down at Steel, who was out cold. He smirked. "Nice punch, Cooper. You and me will have to go a couple rounds sometime."

"I feel like we already have," Bolan said.

Everett's eyes swept over him. "Nice polka-dot shirt. Or is that blood?"

Bolan glanced down at the traces of crimson against the white cotton. "It's from a bloody nose." He smiled. "The other guy's, of course."

Everett smiled back, said nothing.

"Hey, bud," Grimaldi said, "you owe us a hundred grand. Your man lost, fair and square."

Everett switched his gaze to Grimaldi, then back to Bolan. "You two are starting to bore me. Like a couple of real pesky horseflies."

"I guess you don't like to lose any more than Mr. Steel there." Grimaldi gestured down at the bodybuilder, who was starting to come around.

Before Everett could respond, Grimes came up to him. "Sir, we have a problem upstairs," he said.

"Sounds like something might need your immediate attention," Bolan commented.

Everett studied him for a few more seconds, then gestured down at Steel. "Get that tub of shit out of here." He turned to leave, then stopped. "You know what I do to horseflies? I crush them."

"If you can catch them," Grimaldi said.

Everett's mouth drew into a tight line. He turned and walked away. Grimes glared at them before he followed his boss.

"For a rich man," Kournikova said, "he has no breeding."

"No class, either," Grimaldi stated.

"Let's get out of here," Bolan said, pausing to give Ivan's shoulder a congratulatory slap. "I think we've worn out our welcome."

"CHRIST, WILL YOU look at this place?" Everett spit as he, Grimes and two security guards walked through the penthouse. Grimes silently noted that the boss hardly paid attention to the bodies littered throughout the suite. He seemed more concerned about the holes in the walls and the bloodstains on the carpet. Grimes said nothing, figuring the blame would eventually be shifted to him for not planning the capture well enough. It always came back to him.

"Who the hell is that guy?" Everett asked. "Superman?"

"Obviously, he is very good at what he does," Grimes said.

"Tell me something I don't know," Everett barked. "Wait a minute…" He stopped and looked around the den. He pursed his lips and walked briskly to his desk. "Shit. I wonder if he took anything from here. Let me review the videos."

Grimes nodded and snapped his fingers. One of the guards went to the ornate wooden stand beneath the flat-screen TV. He squatted down and used a key to open the top drawer, which held a rectangular metal control box.

The man pressed several buttons on a plastic remote, and the screen flickered to life. About twenty thumbnail images of the penthouse came into view. Everett strode over and grabbed the device.

"Give me that!" His voice was a low growl. He scrolled through the thumbnails, found the one he wanted, enlarged it to full-screen and began playing it in reverse. The picture shifted to a low-light, infrared setting. Bodies danced through a violent sequence of shooting and physical combat. A lone figure in a tuxedo—Cooper—stripped a Taser from one of the guards, knocking the man to the ground and taking out two more. Cooper ran to the desk, grabbed something and sprinted into the hallway.

"Damn it." Everett turned to Grimes. "Would you look at that? He's handling them like they're amateurs. Why didn't you put some good men on this?"

Grimes glanced down at the bodies. "They were good men, boss."

Everett snorted disgustedly and paused the video, ran it back in slow motion, and then tried to enlarge the frame showing Cooper's movement at the desk.

"I know he took something," the boss said. "But the resolution's not good enough to see what it was." He played with the video some more. "You stupid idiot," he snarled at Grimes. "I thought I told you to take him out, not let him walk away with the goods."

Grimes decided it wouldn't be wise to mention that Everett had instructed them to capture Cooper alive so he could be interrogated.

"What did he take?" Everett said, twisting his head and staring at the blurry image. He stiffened. "Shit. He took the camera. The one from the yacht." Everett tossed down the remote. "I told you to get rid of that fucking thing."

Grimes said nothing. He didn't recall that particular

order. The last "fucking thing" he remembered about the camera was giving it to Everett for his perusal. He mentally debated an apology.

"Never mind," the boss said. "This just speeds things up, that's all. Where's the *Xerxes* now?"

"Circling in the Greater Antilles," Grimes reported. "We could go closer, but I'm thinking we should wait for the conference to officially begin, right? Unless you want to consider heading to Miami instead."

"I don't pay you to think, you idiot." Everett began tracing his thumb and forefinger over the stubble on his upper lip. "Puerto Rico's the perfect target. Frying millions of Puerto Ricans during the vice president's visit, combined with our faux Islamist martyr video claiming the territory is a symbol of American imperialism, will force even this weakling we have in the White House to retaliate against the Iranians with a nuke, and my plan will slide into effect."

Grimes had heard Everett describe the brilliance of his scheme too many times. He hoped he wouldn't have to listen to it again.

"Get me the exact coordinates of the *Xerxes,*" Everett ordered. "Is the V-22 ready to go?"

"It is," Grimes said. He'd personally supervised the check of the aircraft earlier.

"Verify that it's been topped off with fuel," Everett said. "We'll go back to the compound now. I'll collect Rinzihov and Monk and take the warhead to the *Xerxes*. Zelenkov can take himself and his men away in the Hind once we set up the nuke and put the ship on autopilot toward the shoreline. He knows how to fly one of those things, doesn't he?"

"Of course," Grimes said. "He's Spetsnaz. They're the equivalent of our special forces."

"You know," Everett said, "I'm getting real tired of

hearing that." He grabbed Grimes by the upper arm and pulled him closer, so their faces were only inches apart. "And you're going to have to take out Cooper and his friends tonight. I don't want them reporting what they found on that camera."

ONE OF THE assignments Bolan had given Tyler and his two associates was to establish a safe house at a neighboring hotel. The one they'd chosen was only a few blocks from the Omni. Close enough to walk to, but far enough away to give them a buffer of privacy. Bolan told the two new FBI agents, Bettinger and Larch, to stay in the lobby and watch for any unwanted company. Ivan volunteered to monitor the back of the building. Bolan then swept their room for surveillance equipment. Finding nothing, he took off his jacket and shirt and checked for injuries. Scrapes and bruises, but nothing serious. Satisfied with his inspection, he pulled on a black T-shirt.

Bolan asked Tyler to go through the camera's memory card. "Let me know if you find anything interesting," he said.

The agent began reviewing the pictures. His eyes widened. "Would you look at this!" He held the camera toward Bolan. "Pictures of our buddy Grimes and some others, along with a bunch of dead bodies. Looks like they were on a yacht or something."

Bolan looked. It was Grimes, all right, and a couple other men, one of whom Bolan thought might be Vince Tanner. They stood around the bloodied corpses like hunters commemorating some new trophies.

Grimaldi glanced at the photos over Bolan's shoulder. "Probably *A Slice of Heaven*," he said. "Right?"

Tyler scrunched up his face. "Huh?"

"A civilian yacht that disappeared about a week ago,"

Bolan said. "Looks like they were taking pictures of Everett's platform rig and got killed for it."

"That's terrible," the agent exclaimed.

"We told you Everett was a bad guy," Grimaldi said.

Tyler frowned.

"We need to get on that platform for a closer look," Bolan said.

"We taking another slow boat to China?" Grimaldi asked.

"Negative. They'll probably be expecting us now." Bolan looked at Grimaldi. "Think you could land a helicopter on that platform?"

"I don't see why not. I saw an old Mi-24 Hind taking off from there when you two guys were underwater. I remember thinking that a rich guy like Everett could afford something better than old Russian army surplus."

"We'll have to move hard and fast," Bolan said. "Jack, can you scrounge up a helicopter?"

Grimaldi nodded. "Acquiring a bird shouldn't be a problem. But things could get tricky if they cut the lights on the rig," he said. "Hard to see out on the briny blue at night."

"Maybe these will help." Tyler pulled out the night vision goggles.

Grimaldi raised his eyebrows and nodded appreciatively. "Kid, I think I'm beginning to like you."

The agent grinned and bobbled his head self-consciously.

"Now that we're one big, happy family," Bolan said, "let's gather the rest of the clan and go get us a chopper."

**12**

Bolan scanned the dark water as Grimaldi piloted the AS332 Super Puma toward the platform.

"What do you think?" Bolan asked the pilot.

Grimaldi pushed the stick forward slightly and zoomed over the platform's superstructure. "Damn," he said, hollering to make his voice heard over the noise of the rotors. "Looks like they've got an M-60 set up on the corner by the landing pad."

"That's better than a fifty caliber," Bolan yelled back. "But maybe we can use a subterfuge."

"How the hell we going to disguise our approach?" Grimaldi retorted. "This tin can makes more noise than a drunken reggae band."

"Let's hope they like the music then," Bolan said. He reached over and grabbed the radio mic, then plucked a piece of paper from the glove compartment and began crinkling it as he spoke into the mic. "Attention, control room, this is approaching chopper. We have Mr. Everett on board." He crinkled the paper again. "Experiencing radio problems. Do you copy? Over."

A few seconds later, a reply came over the radio. "Roger, chopper. Be advised, I have to verify clearance before you'll be authorized to land. Over."

Bolan crinkled the paper again as he spoke. "Attention, control, we are experiencing radio problems. Do you copy? Over."

The banter continued for several more refrains.

"Time to set her down," Bolan told Grimaldi.

Bolan turned to Kournikova, Ivan, Tyler and the two other FBI men. "Remember the plan. When we land, Tyler pretends to be Everett as he gets out and walks toward the stairway, with Kournikova hanging on his arm. It's dark and our reception committee will be confused, so that should buy us a little time. I'll grab the closest guard and have him take us to the control room. We don't know how many personnel they have on this rig, but we're here to recon, not kick ass."

"Too bad," Ivan said. "I like kicking ass."

"And he's good at it, too," Grimaldi said.

"Yeah." Ivan patted the polymer handle of his Strizh Strike One 9 mm.

Grimaldi banked the Puma and began a slow descent toward the large, yellow X on the landing pad.

Bolan checked his 93R, the Espada knife clipped inside his belt on the left, and his minimag flashlight as he silently did the math on their combined firepower. Kournikova had a small Beretta Nano, which had a mag capacity of six rounds. With one in the pipe, that made seven. Ivan's magazine held seventeen and the 93R held twenty, so they were at forty-three rounds before reloading. Tyler and his two compatriots had SIG Sauer P226 Nitrons, with ten and one each. With Jack's P226 nine and his thirty round mag they were up to around a hundred. Not a bad total for first magazine capacities before combat reloads. But they were likely to be going up against assailants who had rifles. The odds, Bolan knew, weren't in their favor, but they still had the element of surprise.

If Everett's men bought into it.

Grimaldi landed the helicopter with the finesse of a master pilot. Bolan looked through the side window and saw two men approaching. Each one carried an M-4 at the ready. He pulled the brim of his baseball cap down and tucked his chin as he got out. Even though the sea was relatively calm, the platform swayed slightly under his feet and a cold wind whipped his face.

"Where's Mr. Everett's regular chopper?" the first man asked.

Bolan pointed past them. "There it is."

As the two guards turned, Bolan lashed out with his Beretta, striking the closest one on the temple. He reached with his left hand and grabbed the barrel of the second man's rifle as the first man collapsed between them. "Release your weapon and act natural if you want to live," he said.

The guy let go of the M-4 and held up his hands.

Bolan jabbed the man's cheek with the barrel of his 93R. "I said act natural. Lower your arms."

He complied. Ivan was already out of the chopper and picking up the fallen guard as if he were lifting a feather. "I throw him in ocean?"

Bolan shook his head. "Sling him over your shoulder for now." He pulled the second guard closer. "How many of you are on this rig?"

"Twelve topside," the man said. "Two dive teams down below, plus the underwater crew in the submerged rig."

"How many topside are armed guards?"

"Two more on the other side," the man said. His face looked ashen in the moonlight.

"You have radio contact with them?"

He nodded.

"Then call them over here now," Bolan said. "Tell them

your buddy collapsed. One trick and I'll empty my magazine into you. Understand?"

The man nodded again and spoke into his radio mic.

After the call was made and acknowledged, Bolan directed everyone over to the shadowed area adjacent to the superstructure. The guard had indicated the others would be coming through the port way, which they did about forty seconds later. The newcomers were quickly subdued. After stripping them of their weapons and securing their hands behind their backs with flexicuffs, Bolan continued his interrogation of the first guard.

"Tell me again, who else is on this thing?"

"Two in the control room," the man said. "Six more below in sleeping quarters. We go in four-hour patrol blocks."

"Well," said Bolan, "you've just been relieved. Ivan, take two men and secure the sleeping beauties downstairs. The rest of you come with me."

Ivan departed with Larch and Bettinger, the guard limp across his shoulders. Grimaldi, Kournikova and Tyler followed Bolan as he pushed the guard toward the stairway. As they crested the stairs Bolan jerked him to a halt and pressed the barrel of the 93R against his cheek.

"These guys armed?"

"Yeah. Sidearms," the man said in a squeaky voice.

Bolan told Grimaldi to check it out. He crept to the window and peered in, then nodded at Bolan, who motioned for the pilot to open the door. Bolan pushed the guard in, then leveled his Beretta at the two shocked-looking men operating the control panels. In less than thirty seconds, both of them had been disarmed and placed on the floor with the other guard.

Tyler's phone chirped. He answered it, listened, then

said, "The rest of the crew's been subdued. What do you want done now?"

"Tie them up and find a secure place to put them." Bolan grabbed one of the men who had been monitoring the control panels and walked him over to the main console. "Show me what we're looking at," he ordered.

"The boss'll kill me," the man said.

"If I were you—" Bolan put his mouth close to the man's ear "—I'd be more worried about what we're going to do to you now." He shook him like a rag doll. "Talk."

"Okay, okay. Those first two cameras are showing the area around the platform. We've got two scuba divers down there with scooters and spearguns."

"How do you signal them to come up?"

"Signal beacon."

"Show me," Bolan said.

The man, whose hands were secured behind his back, turned and pointed to a button. Bolan asked where the divers would come back aboard, and after finding a camera view of that area, sent Grimaldi and Tyler to intercept them. He then grasped the technician's head and twisted it to face the monitors again.

"What do these show?" he asked.

"The submerged platform. It's connected to this section by an umbilical."

That meshed with what Bolan had observed on his previous underwater visit.

"The others show the submersibles and the divers working on the sub—" The man shut his mouth abruptly, as if realizing he'd said more than he should have.

Bolan prodded him with the Beretta again. "Don't stop on our account."

The man squirmed. "Please, the boss'll kill me."

"He's not here," Bolan said. "I am."

"Fine, it's an old Russian submarine. Sunk years ago. It must have been uncovered by the last hurricane. The boss has sources all over the place, and a few of them told him it might be in this area. We've been searching for months, pretending it was for this movie thing."

Kournikova approached the screens and studied them. "It looks like an old Oscar class sub. What is its designation?"

"I don't know," the man said.

Bolan jabbed him again with the Beretta.

"I don't," he said. "I swear."

"Sounds like a whole lot of swearing's going on," Grimaldi said, as he came back into the room, flashing a thumbs-up. "Divers secured. And we've got M-4s and night vision goggles for everyone."

Tyler came in behind him. "We've got them all locked up in a washroom section below."

"You know of any missing subs in this area?" Bolan asked Kournikova.

She nodded slowly. "There was one thought to have sunk in the Caribbean, returning from Cuba, a number of years ago. The K-159."

"Was it armed with nukes?"

She nodded.

Grimaldi and Tyler moved toward the screens.

"Is that what I think it is?" Grimaldi asked.

"It is," Bolan said.

"But it's against international law to salvage another nation's naval vessel," Tyler said.

Kournikova rolled her eyes at him. "Oh, please. Are you that naive?"

Grimaldi began shuffling through some papers in a tray on a nearby desk. He picked up several sheets and brought them over to the others. "This first one looks like it might be in Arabic."

"No," Kournikova said, "not Arabic. Farsi."

"Farsi?" Grimaldi repeated. "Don't tell me there's an Iranian connection."

Kournikova scanned the page. "It is some kind of shipping manifest. The vessel is named the *Xerxes*. They were to deliver a shipment of oil to Cuba. Four days ago."

"Four days," Bolan said. "The ship should be on its way back to the Persian Gulf by now."

Kournikova turned the paper over and looked at some scribbling in pencil.

"There are some calculations here," she said. "With some writing in the Cyrillic alphabet. Distances in kilometers, some mathematical formulas." She picked up the next sheet. "Someone was doing extensive calculations. Maximum yield in kilotons versus distance. EMP blast radius." She looked up.

"I don't like the sound of that," Grimaldi said. "Sounds too much like WMD talk for my tastes."

"Could Everett have taken a nuke out of the sub?" Bolan asked.

Kournikova shrugged. "It is possible. The Oscar class was equipped to carry the RU-100 Veter missiles. I believe your government called them the SSN-16 Stallions. Twenty kilotons. The K-225 was armed with two."

Bolan looked back at the technician, who was sweating profusely. "What about it?"

The man lowered his eyes. "Yeah, but they were only able to recover one so far."

"Where's it at?" Bolan asked.

"The boss took it to the compound."

"The compound?"

"He's got a place on the island. I don't know where. We aren't allowed to go there."

"You should look at this," Kournikova said. "A drawing of an archipelago along with a circle marking variations of destruction is on a subsequent page." She handed the paper to Bolan.

"Where's that?" Tyler asked, looking over Bolan's shoulder.

"Don't know." The soldier snapped a picture with his cell phone. "I'll email it to Hal. Maybe he can find out."

Tyler frowned. "I'd better get on the horn to D.C. right away."

"And tell them what?" Grimaldi asked. "You'll start a panic if we don't know exactly what we're dealing with. Let us handle it through our channels."

"More calculations here," Bolan said, interrupting them. "Looks like mileage versus fuel consumption. Two different listings in English. One is *M,* the other *V.* Mean anything to you, Jack?"

Grimaldi rubbed his chin as he looked at the pencil markings. "That Russian bird's proper designation is the Mi-24 Hind. *V...*" He shrugged. "Can't say."

Bolan grabbed the technician's shirt, pulling the man upward until their faces were inches apart. "You've got about ten seconds to tell me where that compound is before I toss you over the side and let you deal with the sharks."

"I don't know. I swear, I don't know!" The man started crying. "The boss set it up before I got here. Before any of us got here."

Bolan tossed the man back into the chair.

"Do you believe him?" Kournikova asked.

Bolan glanced at the weeping man and then nodded.

"I don't think he knows either," Grimaldi said, his

mouth twisting into a crafty smile. "But I bet I know who does. Le Pierre."

Bolan turned to Tyler. "Get everyone back to the chopper now. We're going to pay a visit inland."

"THE K-225?" BROGNOLA punctuated the statement with a groan.

"You've heard of it?" Bolan asked. He and Kournikova had given each other a wide berth as they walked back to the chopper. He knew they each had to report in via satellite phone regarding these latest developments.

"Only in hushed whispers," Brognola said. "It's on the Russians' missing nukes list. Oscar class sub. Disappeared back in the late nineties, to the best of my recollection."

"Well, it's resurfaced, in a manner of speaking. Can you get the navy down here to take over this platform operation?"

"You bet. I'm going to wake up the President as soon as we finish. What else you got?"

Bolan took a deep breath. "A lot of loose ends and speculation. We haven't located the recovered missile yet. Did Aaron find that address for me on Le Pierre?"

Brognola said he'd check, and Bolan listened to silence for several seconds. "He's emailing it to you and Jack now with a map," the big Fed said when he came back on the line.

"Roger that," Bolan said. "Keep an eye on that Iranian ship, the *Xerxes*. I'm not sure how it fits in, but it has to mean something, and I've got a feeling it's not good."

"Okay," Brognola said. "I'll call back if we have any luck. Stay safe down there."

"Yeah, right," Bolan said, and ended the call. He glanced over and saw Kournikova was off the phone, as well. She walked over to him with a wistful smile.

"Are your superiors as upset over this as mine are?" she asked.

"Probably." Bolan waved his hand toward the helicopter. "Shall we?"

USING THE MAP they'd received from Stony Man Farm, Grimaldi was able to locate Le Pierre's residence easily, and set the chopper down in a vacant field nearby. Bolan told Ivan, Larch and Bettinger to guard the helicopter, and he, Tyler, Kournikova and Grimaldi set off at a jog through back alleys and between ramshackle houses toward the police captain's home. It was on a corner lot, and easily the largest residence in the neighborhood.

"An island of affluence in a sea of poverty," Grimaldi said.

Bolan stopped behind the seven-foot-high wall that surrounded the place, and clasped his hands together, gesturing to Grimaldi. The pilot stepped into Bolan's palms and jumped as the soldier lifted. Grimaldi straddled the wall and did a quick survey with his flashlight. He turned back to others and nodded. Bolan boosted Kournikova up next, then Tyler. Grimaldi lowered his arm to give Bolan the slight lift he needed to grab the top of the wall.

They descended and made their way through the expansive yard, past Le Pierre's in-ground pool. Grimaldi flipped down his night vision goggles and took out his weapon. Bolan removed his Espada knife from his belt. When they reached the back door, they stopped and listened intently.

No noises greeted them. Bolan pressed the blade of his knife between the door and the jamb and gave a quick twist. The door popped open, and one by one they stepped into the house. The back door had opened into an enclosed porch area. Grimaldi went first, using his goggles to negotiate around the furniture. The porch connected to a hall-way with two open doors on either side. Grimaldi poked his head into each, holding up his hand to indicate that it was unoccupied. When he got to the last room on the left he peered in, gave a thumbs-up and lifted two fingers.

Bolan signaled for Grimaldi, Tyler and Kournikova to clear the rest of the house. He stood in silence, his Beretta down by his leg, waiting at the bedroom door. The mixed snoring coming from the bed reaffirmed what Grimaldi had implied: two people sleeping. He made out their forms under the white sheet. A few minutes later, the others returned, and Grimaldi made a circle with his thumb and forefinger. Bolan motioned for him to go inside first.

Grimaldi crept into the room, circling to the far side and removing two handguns from a chair next to the bed. One was a semiautomatic, the other a large revolver. Once he had both weapons a safe distance from the bed, he flipped the goggles up on his forehead and signaled to Bolan.

Bolan hit the light switch and the room was illuminated. None of them moved for several seconds in the sudden brightness. Bolan looked at the two figures entwined on the bed: Captain Le Pierre and Sergeant Gipardieu.

Grimaldi crouched in front of Le Pierre. After a few fluttering movements, the captain's eyes opened and he blinked several times. An expression of sheer terror spread across his face and his mouth opened wide, but no sound came out.

"Rise and shine, sleepyheads," Grimaldi said. He held his pistol a few inches from Le Pierre's face.

Gipardieu awakened, shock and terror twisting his features as well. *"Mon dieu."*

Grimaldi gestured for them to raise their hands. "We've

got some questions for you, and you're going to give us some answers real fast. But first—" he pressed the end of his pistol barrel into Le Pierre's nose "—where's my SIG?"

## 13

Grimes stood back as Everett directed the men operating the Bobcat tractor to transport the heavy warhead up the Osprey's loading ramp. Andrei Rinzihov stood off to the side, acting more nervous than usual. Perhaps he wasn't looking forward to this little nighttime trip. Grimes was glad Everett had told him to stay at the compound. No way he wanted to be within spitting distance of the nuke when it went off.

The boss had changed into a set of black BDUs and had an IMI .50 caliber Desert Eagle strapped at his side in a tactical holster. Napoleon yelling orders at his lackeys.... He looked the part of a general—Grimes would give him that. Even Everett's handgun was first-class: a brushed nickel finish with Aimpoint sights on top and a laser in front of the trigger guard. Grimes silently chuckled at the thought of Everett holding the huge pistol in that Weaver stance he favored, the disproportionate barrel extending outward. Short man's complex again. Overcompensation.

"Be careful with that, you idiots," Everett shouted. The three men finished driving the Bobcat into the semi and began fastening it down. Everett continued to bark orders. He glanced over at Grimes and scowled. "You get through yet?"

Grimes shook his head. "No, sir."

Everett bit his lower lip. "Something must be wrong if they missed both their twenty-three and twenty-four hundred check-ins."

"You want me to send someone to see what's up?" Grimes asked.

Everett considered this, glanced at his watch and shook his head. "No. How many men we got here?"

"Fifteen, including myself."

Everett frowned. "That's it?"

"Well, yeah, boss. We put the extra guards at the penthouse and the rest at the platform and—"

"And they got their asses handed to them by one man," Everett finished for him. He glared at Grimes. "I'll have Zelenkov and his boys secure the platform on their way back tonight. You just make sure you finish that son of a bitch and his friends ASAP. I want them all eliminated. Got it?"

"Yes, sir." Grimes was less than enthusiastic about taking out a group of American and Russian agents, but then again, once the balloon went up in Puerto Rico, killing the vice president of the United States and a couple hundred thousand other people, a few G-men would hardly be missed. He was a little apprehensive about taking on this guy Cooper, too. The man was good. Real good. But Grimes knew he was better. At least that's what he kept telling himself.

"More than likely, the platform's been compromised," Everett said. "We have to operate on that assumption, anyway. Let's just hope those idiots in the control room were able to shut down the monitors if they came under attack. Was there any other info there?"

"The shipping manifest from the *Xerxes,*" Rinzihov said. "I was doing those calculations you wanted on the fuel consumption and the blast radius and EMP range for the explosion." He paused and rubbed his temples with his thumb and forefinger. "I might have left some of those papers in the control room."

"Oh, Christ," Everett said. "If they can figure out the connection between me and the *Xerxes,* I might as well be blown up myself. It's got to look like the Iranians did it."

"Willard," Rinzihov said, a weak grin stretching across his face. "You have set the stage so carefully that a minor thing like that will most assuredly escape notice. After the detonation, there will be chaos and plenty of time for Vladimir and Edwin here to tie up any loose ends." He reached over and patted Everett's arm. "It will be fine, my friend."

"Go get me Monk," Everett said. "Bring him here. Then keep watch in case they somehow find this place. If they do, kill the girl right away. We'll dump her body in the ocean later."

Grimes nodded. That was one task he was looking forward to.

"We'll tie up any other loose ends when I get back," Everett said. "Tell Le Pierre to round up some locals to help."

Grimes was still thinking about killing the girl, savoring the different ways he might do it.

"Move it," Everett yelled. He glanced at his watch again. "We take off for the *Xerxes* in five minutes."

LE PIERRE BROKE DOWN rather quickly, revealing the location and specifics of Everett's island compound. Apparently, the rich man had gone to extraordinary lengths to mask the facility from satellite surveillance. "It is being kept in the strictest secrecy so that his competitors do not see the site for his big amusement park."

"Horseshit," Grimaldi said, pressing the barrel of his gun into the police captain's face again. "And you still haven't told me where my SIG is."

Le Pierre's eyes widened with fear.

"*S'il vous plaît,* please, sir," Gipardieu said. "Do not hurt the captain."

"I won't as long as he gives us what we want. The compound."

"I will take you there," Le Pierre said.

"All right." Grimaldi smiled. "And as for my SIG, I'll keep yours till I get mine back. I always wanted an SP 2022." He checked that the weapon was decocked, and stuck it into his belt.

After tying up and handcuffing Gipardieu, and disabling all communication devices in the house, Bolan and his crew walked Le Pierre through the hot, humid evening to the chopper. When they approached, the two FBI agents were surprised to see the bound policeman. Ivan grinned from ear to ear.

Tyler slowed a bit and tapped Bolan on the arm, motioning for him to drop back. Grimaldi noticed this and shoved Le Pierre at Ivan. "Stow him in the bird, will you? I'll be there to warm it up in a second."

Ivan grabbed Le Pierre and manhandled him into the helicopter. Kournikova climbed on behind them.

Bolan waited until Grimaldi had walked back over to them before asking Tyler what was up.

Tyler's mouth twitched. "I'm having second thoughts about proceeding on this mission without proper clearance from the Bureau's legal advisors."

"Listen," Grimaldi said, pushing forward. "There's no time for that. We got to move fast on this."

Tyler furrowed his brow.

"He's right," Bolan told the agent. "We're going on hunches and suspicions right now, with little solid evidence. But the stakes are pretty high. We may have a loose nuke out there—no telling what could happen. We'll take care of any fallout on our end. If you want, we can make like you were never even here."

Tyler compressed his lips and stared at the ground.

"Tyler," Bolan continued. "We need your help on this one."

The young man's jaw jutted out and he nodded. "Okay, let's go."

ON THE FLIGHT to the compound, Le Pierre became practically garrulous. He spoke rapidly and loudly, saying Everett had approached him months ago about a boat patrol around his movie set on the ocean. If he knew the blockbuster story was a smokescreen covering up the location of a sunken Russian sub, he didn't say it. All he claimed to know was that he and the rest of the island police were paid off so "Monsieur Everett could salvage something he found in the water. A treasure from a shipwreck, I believe."

The compound appeared beside one of the mountains, and Grimaldi did a quick flyover. Everett's stronghold was accessible only via a winding road that branched off the main highway. Bolan made a mental map of the area: front gate with a guard shack, one medium-size brick-and-mortar building surrounded by three larger Quonset huts. Much of the compound was obscured from overhead by camouflaged netting and tarps.

"There's what looks like a landing pad in the rear," Grimaldi told Bolan. "Want me to set her down?"

Bolan considered their options. "We don't know how many men are down there. We need a diversion." He flipped up the night vision goggles on his forehead, then took the microphone from the instrument panel and reached over the seat to grab Le Pierre's collar. He dragged the policeman upward, keeping his wrist under Le Pierre's chin. "You're going to do a little broadcast for us, Captain.

And here's what you're going to say." Bolan repeated the message to Le Pierre, who nodded. When he was satisfied the cop had the instructions memorized, Bolan unfastened his seat belt and turned to Ivan. "You up for a little recon?"

The big Russian grinned. "Recon, *nyet*. Fun, *ya*."

Bolan handed him one of the M-4s he'd taken from the guards on the platform. "You familiar with this one?"

Ivan flipped up his own night vision goggles and took the rifle, looking it over. "*Ya*, NATO weapon. Good, but Kalashnikov is better." He tapped on the bottom of the magazine, stood up and slung the rifle over his shoulder.

Bolan did the same. "Can you rappel?" he asked, holding up a length of nylon and a D-ring.

Ivan nodded. Both he and Bolan used the nylon lines to tie Swiss seats around themselves, and slipped the D-rings into place. They all had the rifles, radios and night vision goggles that they'd confiscated from the guards on the rig. Bolan held up his radio and told them to check they were all on the same frequency.

"Okay, here's the plan," he said. "Ivan and I will rappel down by the front gate. Jack, fly back toward the helipad while Captain Le Pierre makes his announcement. That should distract them long enough for you to make an unobstructed landing while Ivan and I start working our way in from the front. Keep in contact by radio, but remember there are no repeaters, so the range is limited to a few hundred feet. Got it?"

Everyone said they did.

"Don't forget your lines," Bolan said to Le Pierre.

Kournikova leaned forward and took the microphone.

"I will be right here to make sure he does not," she said. With her free hand, she caressed Le Pierre's cheek, then produced a thin-bladed knife from her pocket and held it in front of the Frenchman's face. "And I must warn you, I am also fluent in French."

Le Pierre's eyes widened.

"Okay, let's go." Bolan handed Ivan a coil of rope, opened the side door and secured his own rope to one of the cleats.

Ivan slid open the other door and Le Pierre screamed. "Please! Be careful! I do not wish to fall."

"Somebody strap that son of a bitch to the wall," Grimaldi yelled.

The pilot swept the helicopter back over the compound, then hovered about fifty-five feet above the front gate. Bolan flipped the goggles down on his head, nodded to Ivan, and both men backed out of the open doors, zipping down the ropes toward the ground.

The helicopter held steady as Le Pierre's voice came over the loudspeakers: "Attention, attention! This is Capitaine Le Pierre, Island Police. I have important information for Monsieur Everett and must land immediately."

Bolan landed in a crouch and stepped out of his rope harness. Their descent had put them inside the seven-foot cyclone fence, which was topped with barbed wire. He pulled his M-4 off his shoulder and surveyed the area as he took cover behind a low wall about twenty feet away. Ivan was right beside him. The helicopter circled a few moments more, then headed to the rear of the compound. They heard Le Pierre repeating his message. The guard in the gate shack had his back to them, watching the helicopter and talking on his radio.

Bolan ran the ten steps to the shack. The guard turned just in time to be on the receiving end of the Executioner's rifle butt, and he crumpled to the floor. Bolan stood watch while Ivan searched the unconscious man, stripping him of his weapons and radio.

"I kill?" Ivan took out his knife.

Bolan shook his head. The soldier had no aversion to killing, but avoided it unless the situation required it. They bound the man securely with his bootlaces and stuffed a gag into his mouth.

A voice came over the guard's radio. "Poston and Willis, go meet that chopper. Escort Le Pierre to base. Everyone else stand by your posts. Acknowledge in sequence."

Bolan listened as each guard responded with a position identifier and a "Roger." He counted thirteen responses and whispered into his own radio, "At least fifteen men on base. They're coming to meet the captain."

The guard's radio crackled again. "Front gate, do you acknowledge?"

Bolan keyed the mic while rubbing his thumbnail over the speaker. "Front gate. Roger."

Silence, then the voice continued. "Stay on your toes, damn it."

Sounds like this group is less than highly motivated, Bolan thought. So far we seemed to have the advantage of surprise, but that could change fast.

And change it did as short, staccato bursts of gunfire echoed from the far end of the compound.

Grimaldi's voice burst from Bolan's radio. "We got made. Taking fire."

Bolan and Ivan were on their feet in seconds. The soldier veered right, moving around the brick building. The Russian went to the left toward one of the Quonset huts.

More rounds ripped through the darkness. Bolan reached the corner of the building and scanned the area through his goggles' green-tinted lenses. Three men were firing rifles at the helicopter. Bolan flicked the selector switch to full-auto and zipped them with three crisscrossing bursts. Each man fell. He searched the night for more muzzle flashes and heard the sound of an M-4's steady, 3-round bursts from the other side of the building. Peering around the corner, Bolan saw Ivan engaging two more guards.

Something moved about forty feet to his Bolan's right: a man, also wearing night vision goggles, carrying a rifle. Bolan brought up his M-4 and squeezed the trigger. The man twisted and fell.

"Sitrep," Bolan said, raising the radio to his mouth.

"Shooters at five, six and seven," Grimaldi said. "Ivan's taking fire, too."

More rounds popped in the night.

"Here, too," Kournikova added.

"Cooper," Tyler said, "we're pinned down here in the chopper."

Bolan ran through the darkness, bright muzzle flashes dancing in the periphery of his green field of vision. Ivan appeared to be engaged in a full-fledged shootout at the Quonset hut. Bolan brought up his rifle and fired a burst, then dived forward and did a quick roll. When he looked again, he saw that Ivan had managed to take out his three adversaries.

Bolan glanced to the other side and saw three more men by the farthest Quonset hut, firing at the helicopter. He flipped the selector switch back to semi and zeroed in on the first man's position. He squeezed off a round and saw the figure recoil, then slump forward. The second man paused to check out his partner, and Bolan shot him, as well. A third man ducked back behind the corner of the hut.

"Jack, see if you can secure your area," Bolan said into his radio. "Ivan, let's hit the main building."

He saw the Russian get up and begin a fast trot toward the brick structure. Bolan did a mental calculation.

Eleven of fifteen accounted for, he thought. If there are only fifteen.

Bolan knew that, in combat, there were no certainties as far as enemy numbers until the last round had been fired. He stood and began running toward the brick building. A figure moved behind a second-story window and he delivered a quick burst into the glass. The window shattered and the figure disappeared. Seconds later, a rifle barrel extended and sent a haphazard spray of automatic fire through the broken pane. Bolan easily avoided the bullets and concentrated on reaching the door. He had perhaps thirty feet to go now.

Something moved by the building's back right corner. Bolan hit the ground next to a set of wooden picnic tables, extending his rifle. The movement flickered in front of him again, and this time Bolan acquired a sight picture and fired. The bright flash outlined the body falling next to the wall.

More rounds rained down from the second-story window, chewing up the wooden tabletop. Bolan fired two three-round bursts as he ran. Suddenly, the door flew open in front of him and a man with a rifle appeared.

Before Bolan could react, Ivan slammed into the door from the opposite side, pinning the man and his rifle between the door and the jamb. The big Russian then grabbed him by the head and yanked him all the way out. As soon as he'd hit the ground, Ivan stomped on his neck. The figure stiffened, then lay still. Ivan grabbed the dead man's rifle and pulled open the door. Bolan lowered his own weapon and sent a quick burst into the building. Then he ducked around to the left side, his rifle at his shoulder as he advanced. He knew Ivan was close behind him.

They were in a massive room lit only by moonlight that shone through the windows. The space was practically devoid of furniture or even any sectioning walls, but was periodically interrupted by huge concrete pillars standing like abandoned sentries. A cluster of chairs and some television monitors sat off to one side.

More closed-circuit cameras, Bolan thought. If they'd been monitoring them, they would have seen us coming.

But no one was watching now. He spotted a cinder block elevator tower near the far wall, and a stairwell in each corner. It was as if the building had already been cleared of any superfluous items.

But back to the immediate problem, Bolan thought. Twelve down and at least one more upstairs. He and Ivan paused behind neighboring pillars, and Bolan did an ammo check. The bolt on his M-4 was locked back, indicating an empty magazine. He let the rifle hang in front of him on its sling, and took out his Beretta 93R and his radio.

"We're inside the building now," Bolan said. "Sitrep."

"Rear area secure," Grimaldi said. "It's a hangar. Three men down here."

"West building secure," Kournikova said. "Four more down, as well."

"Tyler," Bolan said. "Take your team and begin clearing those Quonset huts, starting with the one at the rear by the copter."

"Roger Wilco," Tyler said.

Suddenly, Bolan got an idea. He motioned for Ivan to maintain watch on the hallway. Clearing the nearly empty room took only seconds. Bolan went to the television monitors. Most of them were multiscreened and gave infrared views of the grounds. He saw Tyler's group clearing what looked to be an airplane hangar. The only hostiles the screens displayed appeared to be dead. Bolan spotted a blank monitor and turned it on. A split-screen image of the building he was now in became visible. Bolan found a remote and began flipping through different views. One image showed him at the monitors, one showed a single man upstairs crouching by a window, and another depicted a man holding a handgun and standing over a supine female in front of some kind of solid, cell-like door.

Grace Monk, perhaps?

As the man on the monitor turned, Bolan got a look at his face: Edwin Grimes.

The Executioner quickly scanned the rest of the screens. The other rooms appeared to be empty. He clicked his mic once to get Ivan's attention, and when the big Russian turned his head, Bolan motioned him over. He showed Ivan the screens. "Upstairs," he mouthed, pointing to the crouched assailant. He then pointed to the image of Grimes and the young woman. "Basement."

"I take upstairs man," Ivan said. "You save girl."

They left the room and entered the hallway. Bolan stopped behind another pillar next to the stairwell. Ivan signaled that he was going up to the second floor, while Bolan peered down the basement stairs. They looked clear. He moved with precision to the landing and paused again. He spotted a windowless wooden door and a small section of concrete flooring leading into the basement.

Suddenly, a motor roared to life above him. It seemed to be coming from the direction of the elevator shaft. Bolan slipped down the steps two at a time. On the monitor, he'd noticed the basement was well-lit, and he could see a ribbon of light shining from under the door. Shadows bounced in the light.

Someone was heading for the door. The elevator, which an experienced soldier would know was a designated kill zone, was apparently a diversion.

He heard grunts and swearing on the other side of the door, footsteps pounding closer. They were coming toward him in one hell of a hurry. Bolan moved to the side of the door and brought the Beretta up. A quick shot to the back of the man's head as they went by should do it. His main concern was freeing the girl without harming her.

The knob turned and the door started to open just as the sound of gunshots echoed from upstairs. The door clicked shut again and Bolan heard a man's voice.

"Jaros, this is Grimes. What's the situation up there?"

Silence.

Grimes repeated his question, his voice husky. When no reply came, he swore loudly. "Come on," he continued. "We've got to move."

The door burst open, and the girl was thrust through. Grimes was holding her by the arm.

"We're all clear back here, Striker," Grimaldi said over the radio. "They're clearing second hooch now."

The door pushed back into Bolan, and several rounds exploded, splintering the wood. He flattened himself against the wall as the door became perforated with holes. Luckily, the thick wood had warped the rounds' trajectory. Bolan threw his weight against the door and pressed forward. The girl screamed as she stumbled, and Bolan grabbed for the semiautomatic handgun, visible now in the space between the door and the jamb.

The door's sharp edge swung back into Bolan's face, slicing open his right eyebrow. Blood ran down his cheek. He shook off the blow and diverted Grimes's gun upward as it discharged another round. At the same time, he tried to bring his Beretta around through the opening, but he couldn't risk a shot with the girl still caught in the middle. He aimed at the door and fired several times, hoping at least one of his rounds would manage to penetrate.

Grimes pushed the door back at Bolan, the force knocking the Beretta from his grasp. It clattered to the floor. He couldn't release his grip on Grimes's gun hand, so instead Bolan flung himself around the door and collided with the two other bodies. They danced backward in unison as Bolan smashed a looping right into the other man's cheek. The blow didn't have much behind it and Grimes shook it off and snarled, his face twisted with rage.

Bolan's momentum pushed them all off balance and they fell, the girl still sandwiched between the two men. They rolled and Grimes fired the pistol, the round ricocheting off the concrete walls. Bolan still had control of the man's wrist, and slammed the gun hand down hard on the dusty floor several times. The pistol fired again, then flipped from Grimes's hand. He tried to grab it, but Bolan took a fistful of the man's dark BDU shirt and heaved upward. The force of the motion pulled everyone away from the gun, but Bolan lost his balance and fell.

Grimes jumped up and swung something at Bolan's face as he lay on his back. The Executioner jerked his head to the side, avoiding the blow. A leather blackjack thunked onto the hard floor next to his ear. He kicked out with his right foot, catching Grimes in the left side. The blow seemed to have little effect, but Bolan used the split second it took Grimes to regain his footing to roll to his feet.

The two men faced each other and Grimes shot a glance at the pistol, which was at least twelve feet away. He rushed for it, swinging the sap as he ran, but Bolan intercepted him. The soldier blocked the blow and charged at Grimes, executing a perfect over-the-shoulder judo throw.

Grimes slammed onto the concrete floor and his whole body quivered spasmodically. Bolan stepped on the man's wrist, then reached down to retrieve the sap from his limp fingers. Droplets of blood splattered the floor as Bolan bent over. When he straightened up, Grimes was only semiconscious.

Bolan looked to the girl, who was lying on her side, staring at him. He managed a smile.

"Are you Grace?" he asked.

Her mouth opened but no sound came out.

"I'm here to help you," Bolan said. "You're safe now."

He put the blackjack in his pocket and frisked Grimes, then flipped him facedown on the floor.

"Striker here," he said into his radio. "I'm in the basement. Hostage is secure and I've got one prisoner."

"Roger that," Grimaldi said. "We're on the way."

Grimes moaned as he started to come to.

The guy has to know it's all over but the crying, Bolan thought. But it was worth a shot to try and turn him. "Where's Everett?"

"I ain't telling you shit." His tone was surly. "I know my rights. I want a lawyer."

"That might work if I were a cop," Bolan said, leaning down and twisting Grimes's arm up in a hammerlock. "But I'm not. And I don't have time for games."

He grunted in pain. "I want to negotiate."

"You're hardly in a position to do that. Where's your boss?"

"Go to hell," Grimes said, but his tone was less confident.

"I'm running out of patience. It's over for you. We've got all the pieces."

"You don't know shit."

Bolan's mind raced. He decided to try a gamble. "We know about the *Xerxes*."

Silence. At least ten seconds ticked by.

"You've got no idea," Grimes said, his voice cracking with desperation now. "You've got no... Look, I wanted no part of that."

"Tell me everything you know," Bolan said, keeping

his voice placid and calm, "and I give you my word that I'll tell them you cooperated." He eased up slightly on the armlock.

"Okay, okay," Grimes said. "But you gotta believe me. I didn't want any part of it. This whole thing was his idea. He's a maniac. You gotta believe me."

"I do," Bolan said. "Now spill it."

Grimes nodded.

"Time is of the essence," Bolan said. And we've got a maniac to catch.

## 14

"It sounds like you guys stepped into a goddamn war down there," Hal Brognola said into the satellite phone after listening to Bolan's sitrep.

"Let's call it a police action," Bolan said. "We need some backup right away." He heard Brognola blow out a breath.

"We've already got a squad of marines on the way to that platform rig," he said. "Want me to divert some of them?"

Bolan considered this. With the platform secure, this compound was of little consequence in terms of the operation. He'd already sent the two FBI agents, Larch and Bettinger, to the safe house with Grace Monk and the two prisoners, the gate guard and Grimes. Once Grimes started to spill his guts, everything had fallen into place. And then the real race began.

"Have a couple swing by the safe house and assist those two Feds," Bolan said. "What's the President going to do?"

"He's in a meeting with his staff now. We've moved to a high alert status, but between you and me, I don't think he's going to authorize a quick strike on that Iranian ship without definitive verification of the threat."

"Definitive verification?" Bolan said. "Does he know there's possibly a nuke on board?"

"*Possibly* is the operative word," Brognola said. "For all we know, this whole thing could be a setup to get us to take out that oil tanker and provoke an international incident."

Bolan didn't argue. He knew the President was a cautious man. He had to be. "Did you find the *Xerxes* yet, at least?"

"We've got surveillance drones combing the area as we speak," Brognola said. "And satellite feeds, as well. If she's out there, we'll find her."

"Speaking of finding things, Jack found a second Osprey in the hangar. He's doing an inspection now. We're almost ready to roll."

"An Osprey? Didn't you say Everett already took off in one of those?"

"That's what his boy Grimes told us," Bolan said. "Everett had two of them, just in case one went down with a maintenance problem. He's got about an hour's head start on us already, but if he's carrying a four- or five-thousand-pound missile, it'll slow him down some."

"Except you're still not positive where he's headed." Brognola's voice was tinged with skepticism.

"We're operating on the information we got from Grimes, and it makes sense. If the vice president is going to be in Ponce for this international summit, the *Xerxes* has got to be close to the southern side of Puerto Rico."

"That's still a lot of ocean."

Bolan heard Grimaldi's whistle signaling that the preflight inspection was complete.

"Hal, we're shoving off. Keep trying to get us some coordinates on the ship."

Grimaldi was already inside the cockpit when Bolan reached the plane. The rotors were in the vertical position and the rear cargo door was open. Bolan ran up the ramp and saw Kournikova, Ivan and Tyler strapped into seats along the fuselage. Tyler pointed toward the front. "He's waiting for you."

Bolan nodded, continued up to the cockpit and took the copilot's position. Grimaldi handed him a helmet so they could communicate while in flight. Bolan slipped it on and looked at his friend and partner. "You sure you know how to fly one of these?"

Grimaldi grinned. "Does a bear shit in the woods?"

Bolan felt the surge of vibration as Grimaldi fired up the motors.

EVERETT HELD HIS TONGUE as the three men slowly backed the Bobcat down the Osprey's loading ramp. He wasn't about to tell them to hurry, not with them handling something so heavy and so deadly. Funny, the warhead looked more like an oversize Christmas tree ornament than something with the power to change the world.

Everett felt Rinzihov's hand on his shoulder. The old Russian was smiling. He was finally going to get to see one of his weapons of mass destruction deliver the payload he'd designated to his Cold War enemy, America.

Zelenkov stood on the other side, his AK-47 slung diagonally across his chest. This guy looked almost as big as Mark Steel, and was at least half a foot taller. Spetsnaz. That was all that damn Grimes could talk about. Everett wondered how things were going back on the island. He'd wait to use the satellite phone in case the signal could later be traced. He couldn't afford any slipups. Nothing could tie him to this incident.

The tractor's rubber tires squealed as they popped off the ridge of the ramp and slid heavily onto the deck. The three men guiding it froze at the sound.

"Come on," Everett said. "Get moving. It was just the damn tires going down the hump."

The workers resumed their task.

Everett turned to Zelenkov. "Go get the prisoner out of the plane."

Zelenkov nodded and walked past the Bobcat, which was now slowly creeping toward the elevator. Seconds later, Zelenkov dragged Herman Monk out of the Osprey. Monk's hands were cuffed behind him, and he fell as Zelenkov shoved him forward. The big Russian grabbed Monk's arm and lifted him to his feet as easily as if he were picking up a rag doll.

"He's outlived his usefulness," Everett said. "Put him with the Stallion."

Zelenkov cocked his head, obviously not understanding.

Rinzihov said something in Russian and Zelenkov's head bobbled up and down as he steered Monk toward the Bobcat. "He knows it as the RU-100 Veter," Rinzihov said. "Stallion was the designation given by NATO."

Everett knew this, but he liked the name Stallion better. More appropriate, especially in this instance. Like one of the four horsemen of the apocalypse. He glanced up to the navigation bridge behind them, then lifted the portable radio to his mouth, keying the mic. "Tanner, you on the bridge?"

"Roger that, boss."

Everett checked his watch: 2:39 a.m. "What's our present location and course?"

"We're about thirty-five miles away from Puerto Rico," Tanner said. "Still circling."

Things were proceeding on schedule. They'd need maybe another hour to set up the bomb, adjust the timer, program the autopilot for the island and get the hell out of there. A vessel the size of the *Xerxes* would take at least thirty miles to come to a halt, even if the engines stopped. That gave them a comfortable margin of being at least three hundred miles away from the blast—practically back to the island—by the time the bomb went off.

I'll be sitting in my Omni penthouse watching the dawn of a new day for America, Everett thought. A new day where I'll be calling the shots.

## 15

"You want the good news or the bad news?" Hal Brognola asked.

When Brognola's call had come in Bolan had plugged the satellite phone into the instrument panel so both he and Grimaldi could listen and talk.

"There's good news?" Bolan fingered the butterfly bandage Kournikova had put over the cut on his eyebrow.

"We've got a fix on the *Xerxes.*" Brognola gave them the coordinates.

"Pretty much where we figured," Grimaldi said. "I estimate we should be able to intercept in five to ten mikes. Those SEALs ready to help us?"

Bolan heard Brognola sigh. "That's the bad news. The strike force is still at least forty minutes away."

"How far are they from the coast?" Bolan asked.

"We estimate them to be about fifteen to twenty miles out," Brognola said. "And closing."

"What about an air strike?" Grimaldi asked. "I'm sure the air force can knock them out."

"That's under consideration," Brognola said, "but only as a last resort."

"Last resort?" Grimaldi repeated.

"There's still no absolute confirmation that there's a WMD on board." Bolan could hear the frustration in

Brognola's tone. "I know, I know, but remember—I'm dealing with politicians. It takes them forever to decide anything until they debate it to hell and back."

"That's where this whole thing's headed," Grimaldi said. "Have they considered the alternative? If this is a nuke?"

"The President's got a roomful of people trying to figure out what to do, what not to do and how to avoid creating an international incident or a possible nuclear event."

"They'd better get their act together," Grimaldi said. "Or Everett's going to decide for them."

"Please tell me they're at least scrambling some jets," Bolan said.

"They are," Brognola responded. "From Naval Air Station Penascola, in Florida. They can try and sink her if they have to."

Grimaldi pointed to the radar screen, showing Bolan the small outline of the *Xerxes.*

"See if you can get those SEALs to double-time it," Bolan said. "In the meanwhile, we'll let you know about the nuke."

Brognola acknowledged and signed off as Grimaldi began his descent.

EVERETT LOOKED DOWN into the first deck cargo hold as the men were putting the finishing touches on the warhead. Zelenkov was attaching the wires to the fuse. The hold was the designated oil waste storage area, and the pungent odor rising out of it reminded Everett of his youth in the oil fields, of how his father had made him work there to gain an appreciation for the dark elixir from which their wealth flowed. "Earth's blood," his father had called it. And so it was.

Everett slipped his satellite phone back into his pocket.

He'd weighed the risks of calling Grimes, sending out a traceable signal, and he'd decided that he needed to know for sure that once he arrived back on the island, they'd be ready to take out Cooper and the Russians. He wanted to grab some of them alive and find out what they knew, and more importantly, who they'd told. But that was all secondary to the task at hand. Except Grimes still wasn't answering.

Zelenkov stretched the wires from the fuse to the timer and spoke into his radio. "How much time you want?"

Everett did the mental calculations. The ship was thirty miles out from Puerto Rico now, and closing at a rate of twenty-four knots. Setting the timer for fifty minutes would give them plenty of time to escape the blast radius. They would be flying back to the island in the Osprey, which had a cruising speed of 313 miles per hour. More if they pushed it. They wouldn't even be cramped, with Everett, Rinzihov, Tanner and the pilot on board. Zelenkov could take his group of fifteen away in the Hind.

Everett didn't feel completely at ease with the Russians, but he'd need Rinzihov's expertise again if they were able to recover that second warhead from the sub. But Monk was a different story.

Everett looked at him. The man had visibly aged since this thing had begun. He already looked like death warmed over, and he knew far too much for Everett to let him live.

"Fifty minutes should do it," he said into his radio. "But don't start it quite yet. And leave Mr. Monk down there with the bomb so he can see the numbers."

Everett wondered if Monk had heard the transmission. He was resigned to death, anyway, probably anxiously awaiting it. A walking dead man.

Zelenkov, Rinzihov and the others were, too, for that matter, but they didn't know it yet. You didn't sacrifice all your pieces while your opponent still had most of his on the board. Everett had plans to address that task a bit later.

His reverie was interrupted by Tanner's urgent voice on the portable radio. "Boss, we've picked up an incoming aircraft on radar."

Everett didn't like the sound of that. "What kind?" He held up his hand to signal Zelenkov.

"Unknown," said Tanner. "Doesn't look commercial. Seems to be slowing down a bit. Should be on us any minute now."

Had they discovered him? How could they? But he couldn't afford to panic. Not when he was this close. Everett regretted having removed the belly-mounted gun turret from the damn Osprey for weight considerations, but it still had the fifty caliber M-2 on the loading ramp. He scanned the dark sky, saw nothing, then used the night vision binoculars to check again. Still nothing. Then he caught the sound of engines drumming. He focused the binoculars toward the sound, and the source came into view—a plane. No, not just a plane... The oversize propellers told him it was a damn Osprey. No wonder Grimes hadn't answered his calls.

There was only one explanation: Cooper.

It goes to show, Everett thought as he lowered the binoculars and put his hand on the Desert Eagle, if you want something done right, do it yourself.

"No ROOM ON the fantail," Grimaldi said as they made their first flyby. "The old Russian copter's there. And that starboard helipad's got another Osprey on it."

Bolan looked down at the elongated tanker. Men scrambled from a hold near the bridge as an electronic cover slid over the opening.

"That looks like our target," Bolan said, and turned to Grimaldi. "Can you put us down on the port helipad?"

"There is no port helipad," Grimaldi said, grinning. "But I won't let that stop me."

"Okay." Bolan unbuckled his seat belt and climbed out of the copilot's seat. "You back us in and then take off. Put as much distance between you and the ship as possible."

"Bullshit," Grimaldi said, swinging the aircraft around and slowing some more. "I'm in this, too."

Bolan knew Grimaldi's loyalty was unwavering, so he didn't argue. "Okay, get ready to lower that loading ramp. I'll man that fifty."

"Glad we're not exactly toothless," Grimaldi said as he slowed the Osprey and began working the thumb control to rotate the nacelles to their vertical position. "Man, I'm going to hate losing this baby, but I ain't going to take the time to chock the wheels and tie her down."

Bolan slapped him on the shoulder and moved back toward the others. Their faces were grim.

"Jack'll swing around once the loading door is down," Bolan told them. "I'll give you cover fire with the M-2, then follow as you reciprocate. Stay low and remember to conserve ammo when you can. Our target is a cargo hold about three hundred yards aft, right in front of the navigation bridge. Move forward from cover point to cover point using suppressing fire. Communicate your positions with the radios, like we did at the compound. I'll be swinging around the starboard. Try to flank them by taking the high ground. Once I'm in position, we'll have them in a cross fire. Remember we're dealing with a possible WMD, so move quickly, but cautiously. We've got about fifteen to twenty adversaries between us and the bomb. Some of them are ex-Spetsnaz. We've got some Navy SEALs on the way to assist us, but we have to go now and hold the fort till they get here. Any questions?"

No one spoke. Kournikova tapped the magazine in her M-4. Tyler did the same.

The Osprey banked and then leveled out. Bolan felt the craft hover and begin its vertical descent, the pinging of rounds hitting the fuselage like skittering mice.

Sounds like they're anxious to see us, Bolan thought as the top of the loading door began to move away from the frame. He stepped past the others and crouched by the M-2 Browning. Green tracer rounds zipped through the night toward the Osprey as its wheels touched down.

As soon as the door had opened far enough, Bolan started up the .50 caliber machine gun, sending a steady burst toward the superstructure. The green tracers stopped as Bolan rotated the M-2 in a sweeping pattern while shouting, "Go, go, go!"

Ivan, Natalia and Tyler darted down the fully extended ramp. The Osprey shifted to the right and Bolan glanced back toward the cabin.

"Get ready," Grimaldi yelled, opening the port-side door. Bolan continued firing the M-2 until the ammo belt was expended, then lurched forward and rolled down the ramp. The green tracers began zooming by him, but were met with a flood of red streaks from the M-4s.

Too bad it's not Christmas, Bolan thought.

"We are at cover," Kournikova said over the radio.

Grimaldi ran around the edge of the Osprey, firing his M-4 on full-auto. Bolan scrambled to his feet and followed, bringing his own rifle up for a quick burst. Both of them ran to a low breakwater barrier about twenty-five feet in front of them. Bolan flipped down his night vision goggles and saw Ivan, Kournikova and Tyler going over the breakwater wall. He fired off several bursts. Grimaldi did the same. When the others had reached their next cover point, Bolan and Grimaldi made their dash forward.

They veered left as rounds streaked between them. Bolan dived behind a solid fire hydrant and Grimaldi flattened next to a cargo derrick. Two hostiles appeared around one of the pipes, aiming their rifles at Grimaldi's back. Before Bolan could swing around, both men were caught up in a flurry of streaming red tracer rounds as Ivan suddenly came from under the crossover pipes. Grimaldi looked at the big Russian and nodded his thanks. Ivan nodded back and disappeared into the shadows.

They'd advanced perhaps fifty yards.

At least two hundred more to go, Bolan thought.

"We're on the move now," he said into his radio.

Three men advanced from the right side, holding their AK-47s at the ready. Bolan took them out with a sweep of his M-4. The trigger told him he was out of ammo, so he dropped the magazine and slammed in another one. He hit the bolt release, chambering a round, and ran to the place where the three assailants had fallen. They'd obviously come down from the navigation bridge using the raised center deck pipes for concealment. Bolan did the same, working his way to a new cover point. Behind him, the fiery exchange of red and green tracers continued, and Bolan realized he'd almost flanked the first group of assailants. About forty feet away, a man crept between the pipes with an AK-47. Bolan shot him in the head.

Rounds chewed up the deck around him, eliciting a reply of red streaks from Ivan, Kournikova and Tyler. Bolan continued his advance, firing off short bursts as he ran. He got to another breakwater section and ducked down, surveying the area behind him. He'd lost track of Grimaldi.

"Ready to give you cover," he said into his radio.

"Roger that," Tyler said. "Moving now."

Bolan sent several quick bursts from his M-4 toward the last enemy position he'd seen. The other team was about fifty feet behind him. When they radioed that they were set, Bolan ran parallel to the breakwater wall until he got to the end, then vaulted over it, stopping behind the steel latticework of a middeck antenna. He peered through the night vision goggles again, and saw he'd flanked four more hostiles. They were crouching behind a series of pipes, holding their AKs above their heads and firing in full-auto in an undisciplined manner.

Spetsnaz, my ass, Bolan thought as he snapped the selector lever to semi and took out the first two men with head shots. These guys were amateurs. The third one noticed his companions slumping down, stopped firing and looked around. He tapped the fourth guy on the shoulder and pointed as Bolan squeezed off two more rounds in quick succession, each one hitting its mark.

A flurry of green tracers flew toward the superstructure. Bolan saw Ivan moving up, holding a captured AK-47 in each hand, firing on full-auto.

"We are advancing," Kournikova said on the radio.

"We're green," Tyler added. "Using enemy weapons."

Bolan took the opportunity to move farther aft himself, clicking back to auto and firing off more bursts from his M-4.

The deck under him began to pitch and sway.

Must have hit some rough water, Bolan thought, adjusting his balance.

Rounds were zipping by and ricocheting. A sudden grating, metal-on-metal noise interrupted the firefight. Bolan glanced over his shoulder. About a hundred fifty yards behind him, their Osprey had toppled off the raised section of the deck and was listing to the side. The huge ship pitched the opposite way, and when the corresponding shift came about thirty seconds later, the Osprey smacked the deck hard, with more grating noises, before tumbling into the ocean.

Bolan was already on the move again, hoping the Osprey's temporary distraction would give him a little wiggle room. He took cover by a set of perpendicular pipes and checked his ammo. His second magazine was empty, so he dropped it and inserted his third—and last—mag. The bridge was still about a hundred yards away.

Another group of assailants appeared in front of him, running down a gangway. Bolan flattened on the deck and shot three quick bursts into their midst before they could react. Three of them fell, tripping up the two behind them. Some red rounds zipped over Bolan's head and he glanced back. Grimaldi was firing from behind a corner. Two more hostiles fell in a spasmodic dance of death. Grimaldi dropped his magazine and inserted a fresh one. From the looks of it, he was about thirty rounds from empty, as well.

"We've got a low-ammo alert," Bolan said into the radio. "Jack and I are both down to one mag each."

"Roger," Tyler said. "We're a little better off than you. Ivan's been picking up extra rifles like it's going out of style."

Ivan's turning out to be a one-man wrecking crew, Bolan thought. And Tim's shaping up well under fire.

"Advance now," Bolan said into the radio. "I'll cover you."

After the acknowledgment, Bolan stepped up on a metal support stanchion between the pipes, looking for targets. He saw a group of five or six ensconced by a cargo bay about forty yards away. He zeroed in on them and began firing. Two men on the perimeter twisted and fell as the rest ducked down and began to return automatic, but largely ineffective, fire. Bolan continued to spray them until his bolt locked back. He crouched down between the pipes, dropped his rifle and took out his Beretta 93R.

The soldier checked the area in front of him, then advanced, signaling for Grimaldi to accompany him. Keeping low, they ran alongside a series of pipes, pausing for cover at fire hydrants, hoses and derricks, pipe extensions and breakwater walls.

"We're making a move for the bridge now," Bolan said into his radio as he ran. He hoped the others heard him, but if their hearing had been as affected as his was by the firefight, it was unlikely his words were getting through. They sprinted to the raised pipes at center deck and used them for concealment as they continued heading toward the stern. When the pipes ended, they were about thirty feet away from the first level of the superstructure. Bolan paused and looked at Grimaldi, who nodded. Without speaking, the two men ran across the open area and ducked under the overlapping canopy of the second level.

"Let's try for that railing around the side," Bolan said, pointing starboard. He holstered his Beretta, took a running start and pushed off the three parallel rungs of the railing to give himself enough upward thrust to grab the edge of the second level. He swung his foot onto the flooring, then pulled his body up and under the second-floor railing. After doing a quick survey of the landing, Bolan signaled for Grimaldi to make his move.

The pilot took the same running start that Bolan had, but wasn't quite as adept at the ascent. Bolan reached down, grabbed his wrist and hauled him up, helping him secure a solid grip on the metal railing. From there, Grimaldi was able to climb up and join him. They proceeded down a gangway to an open, rear deck area. Bolan noticed a wall that sloped from the third story down to their level. He stopped and climbed onto the railing, turned and jumped, catching the edge of the next floor.

Grimaldi grinned at Bolan, then shook his head. "Who the hell are you, Spiderman? I'll find some stairs."

Bolan nodded and watched him disappear under an awning. This section housed the swimming pool, he noted. Its water sloshed over the sides as the ship continued to pitch and roll with the sea waves. The navigation bridge was one more level up. Bolan could see bright lights shining through a series of rear portholes, periodically interrupted by shadows. The bridge was occupied.

Bolan moved to the section of wall adjacent to the pool. It had two big windows, and through them he saw what looked to be an officers' lounge. He glanced up at the next level and gauged the distance, then took a running start, jumping upward and striking the windowsill with the toe of his boot, using it as a boosting point. This allowed him to grab the edge of a tapering wall that slanted up to the stern. He did a pull-up to gain a better grip, and then bellied over the edge, straddling the wall. The ship was swaying too much to risk standing, so Bolan crawled toward the railing of the fourth and final level. He glanced to his right. The engine room must be below. The sound of pistons grinding was faintly audible.

Bolan managed to grab the bottom rung of the railing and swing his body off the wall. His chest hit the solid shelf below the railing, knocking the wind out of him. He hung there for a few seconds, forcing the air back into his lungs. Then, knowing he had to move, he did an arms-only hand climb, grabbing the successive rungs of the railing until he could roll between them and onto the floor. The bridge was only a few feet away, separated by a solid hatch and a large window.

Someone yelled inside the enclosed navigation bridge—an American, by the sound of it. Bolan took out his Beretta and crept closer, positioning himself next to the hatch so he could peer through the bottom corner of the window. Inside, the area was well-lit, and he saw a man holding a pistol to another's man's head as he knelt in front of the instrument console. A third man stood off to the side holding an AK-47 at port arms.

"We've got the ship's autopilot set," the man holding the gun said into his radio.

"Roger that," came the reply. "Get rid of the captain and meet me at the Osprey immediately. We've got to get out of here now to get beyond the blast area."

Even with the constant ringing in his ears, Bolan recognized the voice on the radio: Everett.

The man holding the pistol shot the kneeling man in the head. He jerked and his eyes rolled back. His face struck the floor with a solid thump. The man holding the pistol turned toward the other one, and Bolan used the opportunity to grab the handle on the hatch and yank it open. The eyes of the man across the room registered shock as he swung his rifle forward.

Bolan double-tapped him, putting two in his chest and then one in his head. As he crumpled forward, Bolan readjusted his aim and shot the second man in the upper back as he started to turn. Unsure whether the hit was incapacitating, Bolan shot him again, this time in center mass, and the man collapsed, his knees folding under him as he dropped to the floor.

Bolan advanced and kicked the gun from his hand. He recognized the face from pictures Brognola had emailed: Vincent Tanner, another of Everett's lackeys.

"Who are you?" Tanner said. His voice sounded weak, desperate.

"U.S. Justice," Bolan said. "Where's the warhead?"

Tanner didn't answer. Three gasps escaped from his mouth, along with a mist of blood.

"The warhead," Bolan said, pointing the Beretta at Tanner's face.

"Get me some help," the man said. "Please."

Seconds later, Grimaldi burst through the hatch on the opposite side of the room, his rifle at the ready. He surveyed the scene. "Looks like you're doing just fine on your own," he told Bolan."

The soldier knelt next to Tanner. More blood leaked from the man's mouth.

"Last chance," Bolan said. "Where's the warhead?"

"Cargo hold one," Tanner said. "Now get me some help."

Bolan stood and looked at the massive instrument panel on the console in front of him. "Jack, do you know how to turn off the automatic pilot?" He went to a first aid box affixed to the wall and removed a gauze dressing.

Grimaldi stepped over to the panel and shook his head. "If it doesn't have a stick or a yoke, it's out of my league."

"You can't stop it," Tanner said, a strange smile pulling at the corners of his bloody mouth. "And even if you could, it'd take thirty minutes or more to dismantle. The coast is less than ten miles away now. You don't have enough time."

Bolan squatted down, pressed the dressing to the pulsing wound on Tanner's chest, and cupped the man's head in his hand.

"Vince," he said. "Where's the rest of the crew?"

"Huh?" The man's face had a dreamy expression now, and Bolan figured the delirium of shock and blood loss had almost pushed him out of reach.

"The crew, Vince. Where's the crew?"

"Cargo hold two," he managed to reply, before his eyes took on the unfocused, sightless look of death.

Bolan dropped Tanner's head, stood up and peered through the window to the deck below. He pointed. "That's got to be cargo hold one. I saw some men scrambling out of it before."

Tanner's radio crackled. "Tanner, where the hell are you?"

Everett.

Bolan picked up the radio and rubbed his thumb over the mic, speaking in a distorted voice. "On the way."

"Rinzihov and Zelenkov are arming the warhead and setting the timer now," Everett said. He sounded breathless. As if he was running. "Get to the Osprey now or I'll leave you. We take off in five."

Bolan clicked the mic quickly to indicate a reply.

"Doesn't sound like we have much time," Grimaldi said.

"No," Bolan replied, "but we have one thing going for us. I'll bet you're one of only two people on this tub who can fly that V-22."

"Sounds like a plan," Grimaldi said. "I'll go take out the pilot and rich man. You go defuse that nuke."

Bolan nodded his agreement as he held up his own radio. "Sitrep," Bolan said into his mic.

"Tyler has been hit," Kournikova said. "I am with him now."

Bolan swore. "How bad?"

"I can't tell. It's his right side. I'm trying to stop the blood."

"We've taken the bridge," Bolan said. "Everett has a group moving back toward his Osprey. I need you to stop them from leaving. I'm going for the warhead."

"Understood," she said. "Ivan will stop them."

Bolan acknowledged and grabbed the AK-47 from the

dead man, checked it and tossed it to Grimaldi. "You go find the crew. See if one of them knows how to stop this thing, or at least avert the collision with the shore."

Grimaldi slung the Kalashnikov and checked the magazine in his M-4. "You know anything about defusing a nuclear warhead?"

"I've come across more than my fair share of these things," Bolan replied. "Every one seems a bit different. But I'm a fast learner."

"For all our sakes," Grimaldi said with a worried look, "you'd better be."

The two men nodded to each other and headed for the stairwell. They stopped at the bottom and stayed in the shadows. Bolan took out his satellite phone.

Brognola answered before the first ring was finished. "What's up?" His voice sounded tense.

Bolan gave him a quick sitrep. "Those jets on the way?" he asked.

"They are, but we're holding off on the order to fire, hoping we'd hear from you."

"How far out are those SEALs?"

"Fifteen minutes max."

"Can't wait that long," Bolan said. "This'll be over in five. I'll get back to you then. If not..."

"Godspeed," was all Brognola said.

Bolan crept up to the entranceway with his Beretta to give Grimaldi cover fire if he needed it. He flipped down the visor and surveyed the deck through the night vision goggles.

Nothing moved.

Grimaldi flashed a thumbs-up and made a dash toward cargo hold two. Bolan waited for ten more seconds, then ran around the massive lid covering the hold of the first one. A sign in Farsi, English and several other languages was posted in block letters. DANGER: OIL WASTE STORAGE AREA.

He pulled up the hatch and saw that the area below him was well-lit. Noxious vapors wafted up as he assessed the staircase into the hold. It looked clear. He began a quick descent with his Beretta ready. The cargo bay was huge, at least a hundred feet deep and seventy feet across. The lower area was filled with rows of drums, and metal scaffolding ran perpendicular to them, creating catwalks along the wall adjacent to the hatch. Bolan saw three men about thirty feet away, on the topmost catwalk. One was lying on his side, his arms handcuffed behind him. The other two were bending over the bucket portion of a Bobcat front loader containing the pointed end of the warhead. One of the two was older, with a professorial air.

Rinzihov.

The other man was muscular and dressed in dark BDUs. He stretched some wires from the warhead to a small box.

Zelenkov.

Bolan ran down the stairs, pointing his Beretta at the men. "Freeze and put up your hands." As he repeated the command in Russian, he saw that the device in the big man's hands was a timer.

Zelenkov smiled. "Ah, you speak Russian."

"And you speak English," Bolan said, motioning upward with the Beretta. "Misters Rinzihov and Zelenkov, I presume."

"You fool," shouted Rinzihov. "If you fire that weapon you'll ignite the fumes and incinerate all of us." He pointed to one of the multilingual signs along the wall: CAUTION! HIGHLY FLAMMABLE VAPORS PRESENT. NO OPEN FLAMES. NO SPARKS.

"I do not think he will use that pistol, Professor," Zelenkov said.

Bolan kept the Beretta aimed at them, but didn't squeeze the trigger. The smell of oil and gasoline was strong, and Bolan didn't know if a muzzle flash would, in fact, set the fumes off. But with the warhead sitting twelve feet away, he did know he couldn't take the chance. He holstered his Beretta as he came down the stairs, and flipped open his Espada knife.

Zelenkov cocked his head, motioning for Rinzihov to back into a corner. The big man pulled out a huge knife with a serrated blade with his right hand, and motioned Bolan forward with his left. Then he pressed one of the buttons on the timer and red numbers began counting down from *45:00*.

"I shall kill you quick, my friend," Zelenkov said, "for the clock, as they say, is ticking."

Bolan circled away from him, sizing him up. He was at least six-five, probably close to three hundred pounds, none of it fat. The man moved with the fluid grace of a bear, his boots gliding over the metal floor in sync with the ship's slow movement.

*44:46.*

Zelenkov held both hands up in a boxer's stance. Bolan did the same. They edged closer to each other. The Russian's knife had the edge in overall thickness and length. Bolan's knife blade gleamed with a razor's sheen.

The distant sound of more gunfire filtered down through the hatch.

"My men are destroying the last of your team," Zelenkov said with a grin.

"Or my team's finishing off yours," Bolan replied.

Zelenkov's knife hand shot out with a quick slashing motion as Bolan leaped away, the blade almost catching him. He thrust with his Espada knife, but Zelenkov avoided the blow with ursine grace.

They danced back and forth, each making tentative thrusting and slashing moves, but neither connecting. In his peripheral vision, Bolan saw the red digits continuing their deadly countdown: *43:34, 43: 33, 43:32…*

Zelenkov's right arm zipped forward again with a quick jab. Bolan tried to spin away, but the blade sliced across his left forearm. Seconds later the tear in the black material darkened and displayed a bright crimson center.

"Ah, first blood," Zelenkov said.

Rinzihov yelled something in Russian that sounded like an encouragement.

Bolan delivered a low kick to the big man's knee. The blow caused him to stumble slightly, but even as he regained his balance he executed a backhand slash with his knife. Bolan ducked under it and managed to run his blade across Zelenkov's left calf.

Both men backed up fractionally and continued their jabs and thrusts.

*41:39, 41:38, 41:37…*

Another of Zelenkov's slicing arcs caught Bolan's right arm, near the wrist. His grip still felt strong, so he didn't think any of the tendons were damaged, but a searing pain came seconds later, accompanied by a rush of warm blood.

Sensing an advantage, Zelenkov jumped forward, cocking his knife hand back and driving it downward in a death strike. Instead of meeting the bigger man head-on, the Executioner moved inside the blow and at the same time thrust upward with his Espada knife, sinking the long blade into Zelenkov's belly under the rib cage. He dodged Zelenkov's knife, then clasped his left hand over the other man's wrist. The two opponents struggled together momentarily, which enabled Bolan to twist his knife in for another deep thrust.

Zelenkov used his superior size and strength to shove

Bolan away. The soldier went flying backward, trying to maintain his footing, but tumbled onto his back as he hit the floor. Rolling to his feet, Bolan expected an imminent and fatal attack from the Russian, but instead saw the man stumbling around in a semicircle, holding his gut, a red fountain flowing through his thick fingers. Zelenkov stared at Bolan for a moment, then toppled to the ground.

Rinzihov ran to the timer. He fell forward, grabbing for it. Bolan rushed over and tried to tear it away from him, but the old man held it fast as his thumb depressed one of the buttons. The red digits raced by in a blur. Bolan slashed Rinzihov's hand with the Espada, then ripped the timer out of his grasp. He plunged the blade into Rinzihov's neck, finishing him, and glanced down at the clock.

*1:10, 1:09, 1:08…*

Bolan scanned for a stop button but couldn't find one. He traced the wires back to the package and a maze of red, black, blue and yellow wires winding around two bricks of C-4 and disappearing into a black canvas bag.

*00:52, 00:51, 00:50…*

Bolan cut open the bag holding the explosive device. The wires stretched to the warhead, where they were linked to another set of wires extending inside the hollowed out portion of the projectile.

That has to be the fuse, he thought. The explosion ignites it, and the fuse in turn causes the plutonium inside to implode, thus setting off the chain reaction.

*00:39, 00:38, 00:37…*

Bolan took a deep breath and looked at the device, trying to decide which wires to pull.

*00:29, 00:28, 00:27…*

Not much time to decide, he thought, but it's not going to make much difference in a few seconds, anyway.

*00:15, 00:14, 00:13…*

He gripped the left wire, the black one, and twisted it loose.

*00:11, 00:10, 00:09…*

He twisted one from the opposite side, knowing if he wasn't right at least he'd have only a few seconds of regret.

*00:07.*

The red digits remained frozen.

Bolan let out his breath as relief flooded over him. His euphoria was short-lived, however, as the sound of more automatic weapons fire filtered in from above. He set the timer down carefully and removed the rest of the wires, then cut open more of the canvas bag until he found the detonator caps. He pulled those out of the C-4 and stood, looking down at the warhead.

Hopefully, the big one will keep for the moment, he thought, stepping over to Rinzihov's limp body to check for a pulse. The man's head was surrounded by a red puddle, his eyes sightless. Bolan then moved to Zelenkov's prone form, squatted, and flicked his thumb across the Russian's open eye.

No reaction.

Both these men are definitely dead, he thought. I wonder how many more are still up there, alive and kicking?

He then approached the handcuffed man. It was Herman Monk, unconscious, his breathing rapid and shallow. Bolan knew they both had to get out of this polluted environment, so he slung the man over his shoulder and strode quickly to the stairwell. The oil and gasoline in the air was making him nauseous, and as he climbed the stairs he thought about how good it would feel to inhale the fresh sea air.

He popped open the hatch and took a quick look around.

Nothing moved; no more shots sounded.

He pulled his radio out of his pocket and whispered, "Jack, sitrep."

"I think Ivan just took out the last of his fellow countrymen up here," Grimaldi said. "What about the nuke?"

"So far, so good. Where do we stand on getting this tub stopped?"

"The first officer speaks English," Grimaldi said. "I sent him up to the bridge to try and turn this thing away from the coast. In the meantime, we were spreading out looking for Everett. Ain't found him yet."

Bolan climbed the rest of the way out of the hatch and carefully set Herman Monk's unconscious body on the deck between the cargo holds. The soldier could feel the steady flow of blood down his arm, and the bandage Kournikova had affixed to his eyebrow had been ripped off. More blood trickled from that wound.

Bolan put the radio to his mouth and said, "Nikita, how's Tyler?"

No answer.

He repeated his transmission.

Still nothing.

"I don't like the sound of that," Grimaldi said. "We're coming up to your six now."

Bolan assumed a crouch. He felt weak, dizzy, but he was sure it was more from the noxious fumes he'd inhaled than from blood loss. He keyed the radio mic. "Jack, what was her last location?"

"She's right here," Everett's voice said from the darkness about thirty feet to Bolan's left. "She was playing Florence Nightingale with your wounded boy wonder instead of keeping watch."

Bolan brought his Beretta up and scanned the area, snapping down the night vision goggles again. The space in front of him turned to a clear greenscape, and in the center, behind one of the cargo derricks, he saw a vertical tangle of two bodies. Everett had his left arm around

Kournikova's neck, his fingers wrapped in her long hair. His right hand held an enormous semiautomatic pistol, a Desert Eagle from the looks of it, with a mounted Aimpoint sight. Not that he needed it, as the barrel was pressed against Kournikova's right temple.

"This is a .50 caliber, Cooper," Everett said. "I'll blow her fucking head off."

Bolan raised his Beretta and tried to aim at Everett's head. The swaying ship made a perfect sight picture problematic.

"It's over, Everett," the soldier said. "Don't make it worse for yourself. Let her go."

"Bullshit," Everett said. "Your Russian ape killed my pilot, but I know one of you bastards knows how to fly that Osprey, and me, him and the girl are getting out of here right now."

"I'm the pilot," Grimaldi said, moving out of the shadows. Ivan stood next to him, and Bolan saw a ragtag group of what he assumed were the Iranian crew members behind them. "Let her go and take me instead."

Everett laughed. "You think I'm a fool? Get your ass over here now."

Grimaldi took a step forward, but Ivan pushed him back. The big Russian charged at Everett, who swung the pistol away from Kournikova's head and aimed it at him. The red dot of a laser sight glowed in the darkness for a split second and was replaced by the flash and roar of the Desert Eagle's barrel.

Ivan recoiled, but kept moving forward. Another gun flash went awry as Kournikova shoved Everett's arm upward. Bolan acquired his sight picture in a second and fired. Everett jerked to the side, as if he'd been hit. Kournikova pushed away from him. He managed to raise the Desert Eagle again, but Bolan's next rounds double-tapped him in the chest and left cheek.

Everett twisted as he dropped, the movement coinciding with a lurch of the ship. He tumbled against the starboard railing, clutched at it, then fell onto his side. The ship pitched back rhythmically, and this time Everett rolled under the lowest metal rung and disappeared.

Bolan and Kournikova reached Ivan at the same time. Grimaldi was already there, holding his hand against the wound on the big man's chest. Ivan puffed twice, each breath sending a cascade of blood from between his lips. His eyes had acquired a dreamy, vacant look and his mouth twitched into a smile as he spoke in Russian, his voice a faint whisper.

"What did he say?" Grimaldi asked.

"It was, 'Goodbye, my brother,'" Kournikova said.

The pilot cradled Ivan's head to his chest as the Russian's eyes glazed over. "Ivan, my man. Oh, shit. Why did that have to happen?"

The sound of helicopter rotors in the distance chopped through the darkness. A Blackhawk zoomed over the ship, banked and swung back around. Bolan saw several lines dropping from the side doors. He took out his satellite phone and hit Brognola's number.

The big Fed answered immediately.

"The cavalry just arrived," Bolan said. "If you're in radio contact with their command, tell them not to shoot us. We're up by the cargo holds near the bridge."

"Sitrep?"

"I think it's about over."

"Roger that," Brognola said. "Give me a minute."

Bolan watched as the SEALs fast-roped down to the deck. They spread out in expert fashion and began moving silently and efficiently toward them. Bolan holstered his Beretta and scanned the group of Iranian sailors for any weapons, but saw none.

"The U.S. Navy's here," he said to them.

One crew member said something in Farsi and the group cheered. They were all smiles.

"Navy SEALs," another loud voice said. "Put up your hands and identify yourselves."

"U.S. Justice Department," Bolan said. "We've been expecting you."

The soldier stood, raised his hands and looked at the young SEAL standing a few feet away. He was clad in camouflage BDUs, Kevlar helmet, night vision goggles, and holding an M-4 with a banana-clip magazine. A SEAL team leader had never looked so good to Bolan.

"One of my team's wounded," he said. "He needs a dustoff."

The SEAL said something into his throat mic, then shot a glance at Bolan. "My medic's moving up the other side. I'll have him take a look. That your injured man?" He pointed to Ivan.

Bolan shook his head.

"I will take you to him," Kournikova said.

"And please," Bolan said, "tell me you have someone who knows how to deal with an armed Soviet nuclear warhead."

"Yes, sir," the SEAL said. "We've been trained for that."

Bolan nodded and blew out a long, slow breath as he looked down at Grimaldi, who was still cradling Ivan's head.

"He saved my life back there," the pilot said, his voice barely audible.

"I know." In the ambient moonlight, Bolan could see how stricken his old friend was. "He went out like a true warrior."

# Epilogue

Bolan, Grimaldi and Kournikova sat in the airport bar, their post-mission drinks untouched on the table. It hardly seemed a time for celebration. An empty chair was tilted forward in honor of their departed team member.

Grimaldi picked up his glass. "Here's to my brother."

Bolan picked his up as well. "To Ivan."

Kournikova clinked her glass against theirs and said something in Russian. They drank. Bolan watched as she fingered the empty glass in her hand, and he wondered if she was going to throw it against the wall as the Russian tradition went.

She smiled, as if sensing his thoughts, and carefully set the glass down. "An old Russian custom, but one best left for another time."

Bolan nodded.

He felt bad about Ivan, but things could be worse. Herman Monk had been reunited with his daughter, and they'd both been transported back to the States, along with the injured Tim Tyler. And the story of their success had hit all the twenty-four hour cable news stations, one of which was playing on the large screen television behind the bar.

"Hey, turn that up, will you?" Grimaldi called out to the bartender.

The man pressed the remote and the newscaster's words became audible.

"...A major FBI investigation has successfully foiled a terrorist plot of unspecified origin in Puerto Rico that was apparently timed to coincide with the vice president's visit. Special Agent Tim Tyler, shown here being transported to Bethesda Medical, is scheduled to be awarded a special medal of honor by the President." A shot of Tyler on a gurney accompanied the voice-over.

"What the hell?" Grimaldi said, his voice drowning out the television. "Opie Taylor getting a presidential medal, and we had to wet-nurse him the whole way."

Bolan grinned. "Well, in our line of work, if you're waiting around for some politician to pat you on the back, you'll have a long wait."

"Yeah, yeah, I know," Grimaldi said. "But I wonder what it'd be like getting a medal pinned on you by the President of the United States."

"Well," said Bolan, "you can always call up Tim and ask him. I'm sure he'd be glad to tell you. You might have to buy him a beer, though. And don't call him kid."

Grimaldi smirked. "He old enough to drink?"

"At least," Kournikova said, "he is alive."

No one spoke.

The news continued with a report about billionaire industrialist Willard Forsythe Everett III, who was reported missing in a helicopter crash in the Caribbean. "Coast Guard and naval vessels are continuing to search the area."

"Good luck with that," Grimaldi said with a grin. "He's fish food now."

"Probably not even enough left for the sharks," Bolan added.

"It is like an old Russian novel." Kournikova got to her

feet. "After much tragedy, justice finally triumphs. Now I must catch my plane."

Bolan and Grimaldi stood.

"Sorry about Ivan," Bolan said. "He was the best."

She shrugged and wiped away a tear. "Sometimes good men must die for the cause. He knew the risks, as do we all."

She leaned forward and kissed Bolan lightly on the lips. "Another old Russian custom. You know, I have to return with our navy to direct the recovery of the submarine." She smiled. "If perhaps you find your way back here we can go for another swim."

"Hey, what about me?" Grimaldi asked. "Don't I get a kiss, too?"

"But of course," Natalia said. She brought her fingers to her lips, kissed them and touched Grimaldi's cheek. "Does a bear not shit in the woods?"

Bolan and Grimaldi exchanged glances and laughed.

Natalia smiled. *"Dasvidaniya."*

They watched as she walked away. Grimaldi smiled and shook his head.

"Just tell me one thing," he said. "How come the good-looking girls always end up falling for you?"

\* \* \* \* \*

# The Executioner
## Don Pendleton's
### ARCTIC KILL

## White supremacists threaten to unleash a deadly virus...

Formed in the wake of World War I, the Thule Society has never lost sight of its goal to eradicate the "lesser races" and restore a mythical paradise. This nightmare scenario becomes a terrifying possibility when the society discovers an ancient virus hidden in a Cold War–era military installation. Called in to avert the looming apocalypse, Mack Bolan must stop the white supremacists by any means necessary. Bolan tracks the group to Alaska, but the clock is ticking. All that stands between millions of people and sure death is one man: The Executioner.

*Available August wherever books and ebooks are sold.*

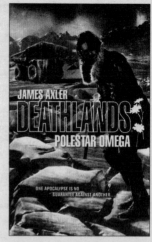

# AleX Archer
# THE PRETENDER'S GAMBIT

### *With one small chess piece, the game begins...*

For archaeologist Annja Creed, a call from the NYPD means one thing:
there's been a murder and they need her expertise. The only link between
a dead body and the killer is a small missing elephant of white jade.

One misstep could mean the end...

**ROGUE ANGEL**
**AleX Archer**
**THE PRETENDER'S GAMBIT**

Once belonging to Catherine the
Great, the elephant was key in a
risky political gambit, but there
is another story attached to
the artifact—a rumor of hidden
treasures. And for a cruel mogul
with a penchant for tomb-raiding,
the elephant is nothing
short of priceless.

Annja must move quickly. It's a
deadly battle of wits, and one
wrong move could mean
game over.

*Available November
wherever books and
ebooks are sold.*

**GOLD
EAGLE** ®

GRA51

# TAKE 'EM FREE
## 2 action-packed novels
## plus a mystery bonus

# NO RISK

### NO OBLIGATION
### TO BUY